Marion Lennox has written over one hundred romance novels, and is published in over one hundred countries and thirty languages. Her international awards include the prestigious RITA® Award (twice) and the *RT Book Reviews* Career Achievement Award for 'a body of work which makes us laugh and teaches us about love'. Marion adores her family, her kayak, her dog, and lying on the beach with a book someone else has written. Heaven!

FINDING HIS WIFE, FINDING A SON

MARION LENNOX

MILLS & BOON

First published in Great Britain 2018
by Mills & Boon, an imprint of HarperCollins*Publishers*
1 London Bridge Street, London, SE1 9GF

Large Print edition 2019

© 2018 Marion Lennox

ISBN: 978-0-263-07801-5

MIX
Paper from
responsible sources
FSC® C007454

This book is produced from independently certified
FSC™ paper to ensure responsible forest management. For
more information visit www.harpercollins.co.uk/green.

Printed and bound in Great Britain
by CPI Group (UK) Ltd, Croydon, CR0 4YY

To Liz and Graham.

With thanks for your support
and love over so many years.
Should we come and build more shelves?

Love you both,

Marion

CHAPTER ONE

'I COULD USE an emergency.'

Dr Luc Braxton perched himself on the end of Harriet's bed and snagged a chocolate from her stash. He was bored. Harriet was also bored but with more reason. She'd smashed her leg during an abseiling training exercise some weeks back. The break was horrific, there'd been complication after complication and she was struggling to regain any strength at all.

'That's not a kind thing to say to me,' she retorted, but she managed a smile. Yeah, she was bored, but Luc took boredom to a whole new level.

Luc and Harriet were both members of Australia's crack Specialist Disaster Response team. They were based at Bondi Bayside Hospital, and while not wishing disaster to fall on the community at large, Luc was edgy when it didn't.

Disaster response was what Luc lived for. Har-

riet's accident, with its possible long-term consequences, had left him gutted, but even the
damage to his friend hadn't taken the edge off
his addiction to adrenaline.

'Was the conference boring then?' Harriet
asked, trying to sound sympathetic.

'Who could be bored in New York? And, no,
the emergency medicine component was great.
I learned a lot. But I did spend most of my time
on my butt, listening, and twenty-four hours sitting on the plane either way. And then to get
home and find the team doing another disaster
drill off in the Blue Mountains without me...'

'Which is why you'd better hope there's no
emergency,' Harriet told him, but there was
sympathy in her voice. Harriet was a specialist intensive care nurse. Luc was an emergency
medicine physician. Neither was good at doing
nothing. 'The team can be recalled fast but it'll
take an extra couple of hours to bring them back
to base,' she said. 'And you know they need to
do it. Our last was the disaster when I was hurt,
and they've been trying to get back there ever
since. They return tomorrow. Let's hold emergencies until then.'

'So you're not bored?'

'Of course I am.' Harriet glowered and winced as she tried to move her leg. 'Give it a break, Luc. I'm likely to be bored for a very long time. At least you can do something about it.'

She eyed Luc with speculation. 'Hey, maybe it's about time you thought about your love life. Word is that cute little nurse you've been dating threw you over before you left. Seems you stood her up for one date too many.'

'Gotta love the hospital grapevine,' Luc said equitably. 'It knows my love life better than I do.'

'You give it fodder. How many's that this year? Three? Isn't it time you thought about settling? Babies and a mortgage and washing the car on Sundays? Not interested?'

'Not in a million years.'

'Word is you were married.'

'Yeah.' He pushed himself off the bed and headed for the door. Personal discussions weren't something he did. 'Eight years ago. I'm not going back there in a hurry.'

'So why the serial dating?' Bored and interested, Harriet wasn't letting him off the hook. 'What are you looking for, Luc? Someone cute, smart, sexy, willing to have nine out of ten dates cancelled because of crises, happy for her guy to dangle from a rope mid-air while the rest of the world thinks he'll break his neck...'

'Harry...'

'Hey, I know, it's none of my business.' She was starting to enjoy herself. 'But you need to quit it with working your way through the hospital staff—it's getting messy. How about you join a proper dating site? I'll help you fill in your profile. What do we have? Six foot two, tall, dark, ripped and just a touch mysterious—or at least he likes crime novels. Yeah, I've seen you reading them between jobs. Super fit. Pulls a great wage. You might need to buy yourself life insurance to cover security issues but, wow, Luc, wait and see how many hits you get. You'll make some girl a wonderful husband.'

'I have no intention of being a husband, wonderful or otherwise.'

'But you've already been one,' Harriet said thoughtfully. 'Want to tell Aunty Harry what happened? Where is she now?'

'And I have no intention of telling you about

my marriage, even if you are bored,' Luc retorted through gritted teeth. 'It's past history. I have no idea where she is now. I'm heading down to Emergency to see if I can find someone to treat.'

'The nurses are saying there's nothing doing in Emergency. There doesn't seem to be anything interesting happening in this whole hospital. Like your love life.'

'You want to talk about yours? How are you and Pete?'

She winced again. 'Yeah, okay, stalemate. But seriously, Luc… My offer of planting you in the middle of a dating site still stands. It might even be exciting.'

'I have enough excitement in my life,' he said, and gave her a hug, snagged another chocolate from her oversupply and left.

Harriet was left staring thoughtfully after him.

'You know,' she said, to no one in particular, 'I'm pretty sure you don't. I'm pretty sure there's not enough excitement in the universe to keep Luc Braxton happy. And I'd love to know what happened, and where that wife of yours is now.'

* * *

Dr Beth Carmichael was so tired all she wanted to do was sleep. Today had been once crisis after another. She was finally free to head home, but heading home with a toddler and a briefcase of medico-legal letters didn't promise the sleep she craved.

There'd even been a drama when she'd gone to pick Toby up from childcare.

'Beth, would you mind looking at Felix Runnard? He's been listless all day and now he's developed a fever. His mum's not due to pick him up until eight tonight and her boss gives her a hard time if she has to leave early. We've popped him into isolation but...what do you think? Should we ring his mum?' Margie Lane, the childcare supervisor, was a sensible woman who didn't fuss but she'd sounded worried.

So Beth had put aside her longing for home and sat down with the little boy on her lap.

A slight fever? The staff had taken his temp an hour ago but now he was burning. He was also arching his head and crying when she touched his neck.

Fever. Sore neck. No sign of a virus. Alarm bells had rung.

'Check his tummy for me,' she'd told Margie as she cradled him, and Margie had lifted his singlet and removed his nappy.

The beginnings of a rash.

Meningitis?

The childcare centre was in the shopping plaza, as was the clinic Beth worked from. She sent someone to the clinic for antibiotics and injected a first dose straight away. She could hope her tentative diagnosis was wrong, but she couldn't wait for confirmation. If she was right, immediate antibiotics could make all the difference.

An hour later Felix and his parents were in the med. evacuation chopper on their way to Sydney. Meningitis hadn't been confirmed but Beth wasn't wasting time doing the tests herself. If the infection was moving fast, Namborra wasn't where he needed to be. It was better to bail out early, maybe even terrify his parents unnecessarily, than risk the unthinkable.

Even after he'd left, there'd been things to do. She'd cleaned herself with care, then organised for parents to be contacted, with antibiotics ordered for anyone who'd been in contact with Felix. Finally she'd stripped again—one thing a country GP always carried was a change of clothes. She'd then hugged her own little Toby and carried him out through the undercover car park.

He was whinging because he was tired. She was also tired, but Toby didn't have meningitis and right now she felt the luckiest mother in the world.

'Let's have spaghetti for tea,' she told Toby, and his little face brightened.

'Worms.'

'Exactly. How many worms would you like?'

'One, two, a hundred,' he crowed, and buried his head in her shoulder.

She hugged him tight and headed toward the entrance. Doug, her next-door neighbour, would be waiting to pick her up. Bless him, she thought, not for the first time. Doug was in his seventies, a widower who spent his days making his garden and his car pristine. When she'd first started working at Namborra he'd noticed the number of taxis she was using and tentatively made his offer. At first she'd been reluctant—her hours were all over the place—but she'd finally accepted that Doug's offer filled a need for him as well as for her.

Giving was lovely. She'd realised that a long time ago. It was the taking that was the hardest.

So now...she'd kept Doug waiting for over an hour but she couldn't hurry. The light was dim and she had trouble making out the pillars. Grey on grey was her worst-case scenario.

Sometimes she even conceded a cane would help.

'Yeah, a toddler in one arm, a holdall and briefcase in the other plus a cane...where? Not going to happen...'

And then she paused.

There was a roaring from above, the sound of a plane.

The town's small airstrip was close. It wasn't so unusual for planes to fly overhead, but the approaching roar was so loud it was making the building vibrate.

What the...?

She had a fraction of a second to clutch Toby tighter and duck because that was what she always did when she sensed trouble. Keep your head out of the firing line…

All of her was in the firing line. So was all of the Namborra Plaza.

Luc had finally found something to do. A kid playing hockey after school, no shin pads and a ball hit with force. He'd been bleeding impressively as his teacher had tugged him through the emergency doors. The dressing they'd hopefully taped to his lower leg wasn't doing it.

The kid was ashen and feeling nauseous, mostly from the sight of blood rather than the pain, Luc thought, but eight stitches, a neat dressing and a promise of a scar had him restored to boisterous. 'You're sure it'll scar?' he demanded.

'Just a hairline,' Luc told him.

'You can't make it bigger?'

Luc grinned. 'You want me to re-stitch, only looser?'

The kid chuckled. A nurse appeared with soda

and a sandwich and the kid attacked them as if there was no tomorrow.

'Shin guards from now on,' Luc told him, and then the beeper in his pocket vibrated.

The hospital used his phone—or the intercom—to page him. The vibrating pager was used for members of the Specialist Disaster Response.

Three buzzes, repeated.

Code One.

Yes!

Or…um…no. He shouldn't react like this. Code One emergencies meant the highest level of need. It meant that somewhere people were in dire trouble. He should hate it, and a part of him did. After a multiple casualty event, he made use of the SDR's debriefing service and sometimes even that didn't stop him lying awake in the small hours, reliving nightmare scenarios.

But this was what he was trained for, and in a way it was what he needed.

One of the team's more perceptive psychologists had had a go about it once, and for some reason—the nightmares must have been bad—he'd let her probe.

'Your childhood was traumatic and your mum depended on you?' In typical psych. fashion she'd put it back on him. 'How did that make you feel?'

And for some reason he'd let himself think about it.

His mother had walked out on his father when he'd been a toddler. She'd gone from one tumultuous relationship to another, one crisis to another. His earliest memories... 'Is there anything in the fridge? Go next door and ask Mrs Hobson for something. Tell her I'd kill for a piece of toast. And aspirins. Go on, Luc, Mummy will hug you if you get her an aspirin...'

More dramatically, he remembered a drunk and angry boyfriend tossing them out at midnight. He remembered his aunt arriving and scolding him. 'What are you doing, boy, standing round doing nothing? Go back inside and demand he give your mother her belongings. Go on, Luc, he won't hit *you*. Can't you see your mother needs you? You're no use to anyone if you can't help.'

He'd been seven years old. Somehow he'd

faced down his mother's bullying boyfriend. He'd pushed what he could see into a suitcase and his aunt had reluctantly taken them in.

And then there'd been his cousin…

Don't go there.

'So you've always associated love with being needed?' the psychologist had asked, but it was too close to the bone and Luc had ended the sessions.

Did he associate dependence with love? There was a germ of truth, he acknowledged, and maybe that's why he and Beth…

But this was no time to think of his failed marriage. His pager was still buzzing.

Don't run in the hospital.

His long-legged stride came close.

After the massive roar of the plane, the shock of impact, then the domino effect as the slabs of concrete smashed down around them, there was suddenly silence.

And then the car alarms started, reacting to the fall of debris.

Beth was on the ground—at least she thought

it was the ground. Her back was hard against a pillar.

There was rubble all around her, almost head-high.

Something was across her leg. Something…

The pain was unbelievable.

But worse… Toby was silent.

The air was so thick she could hardly breathe. Toby.

She was still cradling him against her chest. His little body was curved into hers.

His stillness…

'Toby…' Her voice came out as a strangled, dust-choked whisper. 'Toby?'

And he moved, just a fraction, to bury his face deeper into her breast. A whimper…

Thank you. Oh, thank you.

Her hands were moving over him, searching, pushing away rubble.

No blood. No more whimpers as she ran her fingers over his body.

She was good at this, assessing in the dark. Too good. But her skill was useful now. Her fingers were telling her there seemed no damage. Her arms had been around his chest and his head. He seemed okay.

But for herself…

There was no damage to her hands—maybe scratches but nothing serious. But her leg…

She tried to pull it free from the rubble, and the pain that shot through her body was indescribable.

But Toby was her priority. She was wearing a T-shirt, the one she'd changed into in a rush after treating Felix. Somehow she managed to put Toby back from her, enough to wiggle the hem of the T-shirt up to her neck. Then she pulled it down again, all the way over Toby, turning it into a cocoon to protect him from the dust.

Still he didn't move. The noise, the shock, the darkness must have sent him into panic and for most toddlers the reaction to blind panic was to freeze.

'It's okay,' she whispered, but it wasn't.

Breathing seemed almost impossible. Her mouth was full of grit. The dust wasn't settling.

Toby was safe under her T-shirt, but what was the rule? In a crisis, first ensure your own safety. You're no use to anyone if you're dead.

Okay, Toby had come first but now she needed to focus on herself.

The leg… She needed to…

Breathe. That was top of the list.

She was cradling Toby with one arm. With the other she groped and found the canvas carryall she'd brought from crèche. The clothes she'd just taken off were in a plastic bag on the top. Maybe they were contaminated with meningitis virus but now wasn't the time to quibble.

Oh, her leg…

Somewhere close by, someone started to scream.

There was nothing she could do about it.

First save yourself.

She'd been wearing a blouse when she'd treated Felix and it was at the top of the bag. She tugged it free and a flurry of concrete rubble fell into the bag as she pulled it out.

Was there anything around her likely to fall? How could she tell?

The darkness was total. Her phone had a torch but her phone was at the bottom of her purse and where was her purse? Not within reach.

No matter. She was used to the dark.

Toby wasn't, though. He was whimpering, his little body shaking.

There was nothing she could do until she had herself safe.

She had the shirt free. She shook the worst of the dust out, knowing more was settling every second. Then she had to let Toby go while she wrapped and tied the shirt around her face.

The whimpering grew frantic.

'It's okay.' And blessedly it was. The shirt made breathing not easy but at least possible.

She took a moment to cradle Toby again, hugging him close, blocking out the messages her leg was sending her.

'Stay still, Toby, love,' she whispered. 'I need to see if I can get this...this mess away from us so we can go home.'

Fat chance. She wasn't going anywhere soon. Oh, her leg...

Was she bleeding? She couldn't tell and she had to know.

Carefully she manoeuvred Toby around to her side, though he clutched her so hard she had to tug. Thankfully the neck of her T-shirt was tight so he was safe enough in there. He wasn't crying loudly—just tiny terrified whimpers that did something to her heart.

But her leg had priority. With Toby shifted to the side she could lean down and feel.

There was a block of concrete lying straight across her lower leg. Massive. She couldn't feel either end of it.

She was bent almost double, fighting to get her fingers underneath, fighting to see if there was wriggle room.

Her fingers could just fit under.

No blood or very little. She wasn't bleeding out, which was kind of a relief.

The pain was…was…there were no words.

She went back to clutching Toby. If she just held on…

She was awash with nausea and faintness. The darkness, the pain, the fear were almost overwhelming and the temptation was to give in. She could just let go and sink into the darkness.

But that'd mean letting go of Toby. He was being so still. Why? She didn't have room in her head to answer. He was breathing, his warm little body her one sure thing in this nightmare.

The sound from the car alarms was appalling. The screaming from far away reached a crescendo and then suddenly stopped, cut off.

There was nothing she could do. Her world was confined to dark and dust and pain—and Toby.

There was nothing else.

Even without the emergency code, Luc would have known there was trouble the moment he walked into the Specialist Disaster Response office. Mabel, the admin secretary, was staring at the screen and her fingers were flying over the keyboard. This was what she was trained for.

Mabel sensed rather than saw him arrive, and she didn't take her eyes from the screen as she spoke.

'Plane crash into shopping centre,' she said over her shoulder. 'Cargo plane. Pilot on board but hopefully no passengers. It's smashed into the side of the Namborra Shopping Plaza. You know Namborra? Five hours' drive inland, due west. It's the commercial centre for a huge rural district. Hot day, air-conditioned shopping centre, Tuesday afternoon. There's no word yet but guess is multiple casualties. It seems the undercover car park and a small section of the plaza itself have collapsed.'

'What resources are on the ground?' Luc asked.

'There's a small local hospital but anything serious gets airlifted here, so there are few resources. I'm bringing the team back, field hospital, the works, but it'll take time to get them there. Luc, I'm trying to sequester med staff from the rest of the hospital but they're not geared up like you are. The fire team's already notified and the first responders will go with you. The chopper's on the roof. Gina's refuelling and ready to go. Resources will follow at need but I want you in the air ten minutes ago. Go!'

And ten seconds later he was gone.

CHAPTER TWO

'MESS' DIDN'T BEGIN to describe what was beneath them.

From the air Namborra looked what it was, a small, almost-city situated in the middle of endless miles of wheat fields. There was a railway line and station, and a massive cluster of wheat silos. A group of commercial buildings formed the town centre, with a mammoth swimming pool and sports complex to the side. But Luc's focus was on the largest building of all—a vast, sprawling undercover shopping plaza.

The scene of disaster.

The plane seemed to have skimmed across the rooftop, bringing part of the roof down and then smashing into the sports oval next door. That was some consolation, he thought, but not much. He couldn't see the plane—what he saw was a smouldering mess.

And the plaza... There was a local fire engine

on site, with men and women doing their best to quench a small fire smouldering a third of the way across the smashed roof. There were two police cars.

There were locals, visibly distressed even from where Luc gazed from the chopper, some venturing out onto the collapsed roof, others clustering around people on the ground. Some were simply clutching each other.

They circled first. Gina, the team's pilot, knew the drill. Even though seconds counted, there was always the need to take an aerial assessment. Calculate risks.

'Hard hats. Full gear. You know the drill,' Kev, the burly chief of the SDR fire crew, barked. 'Anyone going in under that mess, watch yourself.' He was including Luc in his orders. SDR medics were supposed to stay on the sidelines and treat whoever was brought to them but it often didn't work that way. In truth firefighters often ended up doing emergency first aid and the medics often ended up digging or abseiling or whatever. No one asked questions—in a crisis everyone did what they had to do.

'Obey orders and keep your radios close,' Kev

ordered as the chopper landed. 'Back-up's on its way but it'll take time. For now there's just us. Okay, guys, let's go.

Toby was recovering from the initial shock. Blessedly he didn't seem hurt. One little hand wriggled free, up through the neck of her T-shirt. Tiny fingers touched her neck, reaching up to her cheek. She wiped the grit away as best she could. Toby was making sure it was her.

'M-Mama...'

There were car alarms sounding all around her, a continuous screaming she couldn't escape from, but she heard...or maybe she felt him speak. Toby had been calling her Mama for two months now and every time she heard it her heart turned over. Now, in the midst of noise and pain and fear...no, make that noise and pain and terror, it still had the capacity to ground her.

This little person was the centre of her universe and she wasn't about to let a crushed leg and a shopping centre fallen down around her make her forget that.

'It's okay, Toby, love.' Could he hear above the cacophony? She had to believe he could. Maybe like her, he could feel her voice. She fought to fumble her way into her bag, until her fingers closed on a scrappy, chewed rabbit.

Robert Rabbit was incongruously purple, so garish that even Beth could usually make him out in dim light. She couldn't make him out now—the darkness was absolute—but she felt his scrappy fur and he gave her inexplicable comfort.

She'd be okay. They'd be okay.

If only her head didn't feel…fuzzy. If only the noise would stop and the waves of pain would recede.

She pushed them away—the pain and the faintness—and focussed hard on Toby. And Robert. She put the scraggy rabbit into the little hand and tucked both hand and rabbit back down her T-shirt.

There was one blessing in all this. Because she'd been delayed at childcare, one of the women had given Toby warm milk and changed him into his pyjamas. She'd intended to heat spaghetti at home. Toby would have eaten a few 'worms' and then he'd have crashed. He didn't really need the spaghetti, though. He'd had a full day of childcare. It was dark, he was well fed and he was tired. With luck he'd sleep.

'Heydee, heydee-ho, the great big elephant is so slow...'

The simple child's song was one she used to settle him in the middle of the night, rocking him, telling him all was well in his world, all was well in her world. She forced herself to croon it now.

The car horns were blaring but he must be able to feel her singing. He was so close. A heartbeat...

'He swings his trunk from side to side, as he takes the children for a ride...'

Her throat was caked with dust but somehow she managed it. And she managed to rock, just a little, with both hands cradling Toby.

'Heydee, heydee-ho...' Oh, it hurt. Dear God... If she fainted. *'Heydee...'*

And blessedly she felt him relax. This had been scary for a few moments but now...maybe it was no worse than being put into his own cot in his own room. He had his mama. He had his rabbit. He was…safe?

If only she could believe that.

Toby snuggled deeper as she held him and tried to take comfort in him. The shards of pain were growing stronger. The faintness was getting closer…

Do not give in.

'Heydee…'

He needed his team!

There was a local paramedic team onsite, plus another from a small town twenty minutes' drive away, but they didn't have the skills, equipment or know-how to try and go underneath the mess. There seemed to be only one available local doctor. She was working flat out in the nearby hospital. That meant triage and immediate life-saving stuff was up to Luc.

A café at the outer edge of the plaza had collapsed, with a group of senior citizens inside, and that's where the firefighters centred their early rescue efforts. One dead, two injured. Luc was in there until the café was cleared, crawling under the rubble to set up intravenous IVs and pain relief.

He was filthy. A scrape on his cheek was bleeding but as the last gentleman was pulled from the rubble he was already looking around for what needed doing next.

There were still no-go areas, smouldering fires, a mass of collapsed tiles where the plaza proper started.

Where to start…

'We're going into the car park.' Kev had been supervising the final stages of freeing the senior cits and he was now staring out at the flattened roof of what had been the undercover parking lot. It was a mass of flattened sheets of corrugated iron and the remains of concrete pillars.

'How the hell did that collapse?' Luc muttered, awed.

'Minimal strength pillars,' Kev commented. 'Concrete that looks like it'll last for ever but turns to dust. The plane's gone in across the top and they've come down like dominoes.'

'Any idea how many under there?'

'We hope not many.' At Luc's look of surprise he shrugged. 'Tuesday's not a busy shopping day. It's too late for after-school shopping, too early for the place to be closing. Most were either in the plaza itself or had gone home. The locals pulled a couple out from the edges but there's reports of a few missing. Don and Louise Penbroke, mah-jong players extraordinaire, had just left the café when it hit. Bill Mickle, a local greyhound racer. One of the local docs...'

'A doctor...' It shouldn't make a difference. It didn't, but still...

'Young woman doctor, works at the clinic,' Kev told him. 'Just picked her kid up from childcare. Her driver was supposed to meet her at the entrance—he's yelling to anyone who'll listen that she's trapped under there. So that's four definites but possibly more. Hell, I wish we could get those car alarms off. To be stuck underneath with that racket...they won't even hear us if we yell.'

Her world was spinning in tighter circles where only three things mattered. Taking one breath after another. That was important. Cradling Toby's small warm body. If he wasn't here, if she'd dropped him, if she couldn't feel his deep, even breathing, she'd go mad. And the pain in her leg…

But she would hold on. If she fainted she might drop Toby. He might crawl away. He was her one true thing and for now she was his.

Dear God, help…

Please…

The firefighters were lifting one piece of iron after another, working with infinite care, taking all the trouble in the world not to stand where people might be lying underneath, not to cause further falls, not to cause dust that might choke anyone trapped.

They found Don and Louise Penbroke first. The third sheet of iron was raised and the elderly couple looked like the pictures Luc had seen of petrified corpses from Pompeii, totally still, totally covered, the only difference being they were covered in concrete dust and not ash.

But as the first guy to reach them touched a debris-coated shoulder there was a ripple of movement. Still clutching each other, the couple managed to sit up. Louise had her face buried in Don's chest and Don's face was in Louise's thick white hair.

Within seconds Luc had their faces cleared. They still clutched each other, their eyes enormous.

'Th-thank…' Don tried to speak but Luc put his hand on his shoulder and shook his head. And smiled.

'You two should thank each other. That's the best way to survive I've seen. What hurts?'

But amazingly little did. They'd been by the ramp leading up to the car park, protected by the concrete sides. They were both shocked but fine.

One happy ending.

A couple of the firies steered them out into the afternoon sunshine where they were greeted with tears and relief.

The firies—and Luc—worked methodically on.

There had to be some way to turn those damned car alarms off, Luc thought. There were fractions of time between the blaring but never enough to call and receive a warning.

At least batteries were starting to fail. The barrage of sound was lessening.

Another sheet came free.

Hell.

This guy hadn't been so lucky. A sheet of iron had caught him. He'd have bled out almost instantly, Luc thought, and wondered how many others were to be found. They were waiting for proper machinery to search the crumpled part of the plaza itself. How many...?

And then...a cry?

The sound was from their left, heard between car sirens.

Kev demanded instant stillness. The sound had come from at least three sheets of iron across. If they went for it, they risked crushing others who lay between.

They waited for another break in the alarms. Kev ordered his team to spread out to give a better chance of pinpointing location.

'Call if you can hear us?' Kev yelled.

'H-here.'

A woman's voice. Faint.

A roofing sheet was pulled up, the rubble lifted with care but with urgency. It revealed nothing but crushed concrete. These pillars were rubbish.

Someone's head would roll for these, Luc

thought. They looked as if they'd been built with no more idea of safety standards than garden statuary.

He was heaving rubble too, now. By rights he should be out on the pavement, treating patients as they were brought to him, but with the local doctor working in the nearby hospital he'd decided the urgent need was here. If there was something major the paramedics would call him back.

All his focus was on that voice. That cry.

'Stop,' Kev called, and once again he signalled for them to stand back and locate.

And then... The voice called again, fainter.

This area held the worst of the crushed concrete. Sheets of roofing iron had fallen and concrete had crumpled and rolled on top. They were working from the sides of each sheet, determined not to put more weight on the slab.

'Please...' The sirens had ceased again for a fraction of a moment and the voice carried upward. She must be able to hear them. She was right...here?

Others had joined them now, hauling concrete away with care. Half a dozen men and women, four in emergency services uniforms, two burly locals, all desperate to help.

'Reckon it's the doc.' One of the locals spoke above the noise. 'Hell, it's the doc. We gotta get—'

His words were cut off again by the car alarms, but the urgency only intensified.

And finally the last block of concrete was hauled clear. The sheet of iron was free to be shifted.

Willing hands caught the edges. Kev was there, taking in the risks, assessing to the last.

'Lift,' he said at last. 'Count of three, straight up...'

And the iron was raised and moved aside.

Revealing a woman huddled underneath.

Luc was underneath before the iron was clear. He was stooping, feeling his way in, reaching her. He was lifting a cloth she'd obviously used to protect her face, wiping her face free, clearing her airway. He had a mask on her almost instantly. The initial need was clean air, more important than anything else.

She was matted with grey-white dust. Her eyes were terrified. 'My...my baby...'

And then she faltered as she stared wildly into his eyes. Even with his mask, even with the dust, she knew him.

'Luc?'

He felt as if all the air had been sucked from his body.

Beth!

His wife.

Not his wife. She'd walked away eight years ago. For a while he'd tried to keep in touch but it had been too hard for both of them.

'Stay safe.' That had been Beth's last ask of him. 'I know you can't keep out of harm's way but, oh, Luc, don't you dare get yourself killed.'

And she'd touched his face one last time, and climbed aboard a train bound for Brisbane.

Stay safe. What a joke, when here she was, trapped by a mass of rubble, so close to death....

The nearest car alarm stopped abruptly. In reality its battery had probably died, but to Luc it felt like the world had stopped. Instinctively his hand came up to adjust his own mask, a habit entrenched by years of crisis training.

His mask was fine. His breathing was okay.

And he wasn't hallucinating.

Beth…

'Leg trapped,' Kev at his side murmured, and just like that, the doctor in Luc stepped in. Thankfully, because the rest of him was floundering like a stickleback out of water.

'You're going to be okay,' he told her, in a voice he could almost be proud of. It was the voice he was trained to use, strong, sure, with a trace of warmth, words to keep panic at bay.

He needed to get the whole picture. He leaned back a little so he could see all of her.

She was slumped against the remains of a pillar. There was a mound under her shirt, and she was cradling it with both hands. A slab of concrete had fallen over her left leg. Her right leg was tucked up, as if she'd tried to haul back at the last minute, but he couldn't see her left foot.

His gaze went back to her face, noting the terror and the pain, then his gaze moved again to the mound at her chest. A child?

He put a hand on the mound and felt a wash of relief as he registered warmth and deep, even breathing. He slipped a hand under her T-shirt and located one small nose. Clear. Beth had managed to protect the airway.

Beth's child?

This was sensory overload, but he had to focus on imperatives.

'Your baby?' he said, because the fact that a child was breathing didn't necessarily mean all was well.

'T-Toby.'

'Toby,' he said, and managed a smile. 'Great name. Beth, was Toby hit? Do you know if he's been hurt?' He lifted the mask a little to let her speak.

'I felt… I felt the fall.' Her voice was a hoarse whisper, muffled by the mask. 'I crouched. Toby was under me. He seems fine. He's fallen asleep and I'm… I'm sure it's natural. It's been…it's been a big day at childcare.'

'Huge,' he agreed. He was acting on triage imperatives, taking her word for the child's safety for the moment as he moved his hands down to her leg. The dust was a thick fog the light was having trouble penetrating. He winced as he reached her ankle and could feel no further.

'It's…stuck…' Beth managed.

'Well diagnosed, Dr Carmichael,' he said, and she even managed a sort of smile.

'I'm good.'

'I suspect you've been better. Pain level, one to ten?'

'S-Six.'

'Honest?'

'Nine, then,' she managed, and then decided to be honest. 'Okay, ten.'

And she wouldn't be exaggerating. He looked at the slab constricting her leg and he felt sick. She'd been under here for more than an hour. Maybe two. What sort of long-term damage was being done?

There was no use going down that road. Just do what came next.

'Relief coming up now,' he said, loading a syringe. There were workers all around them now, shoring rubble. Kev was making his workplace as secure as he could, but Luc was noticing nothing but Beth. If he couldn't block out fears for personal safety then he shouldn't be here. 'No allergies?' He should know that. He did but he wasn't trusting memory. He was trusting nothing.

'N-no.'

'What else hurts, Beth?'

'I… My back…'

She was sitting hard against concrete, as if she'd been slammed there. She had full use of her arms and fingers, he could see it in the way she cradled the bundle on her breast. But what other damage?

First things first.

He should get the child… Toby…away to where he could be examined properly, where he was safe, but for now she was clutching him as if her own life depended on that hold. She was holding by a faint thread, he thought, and he wasn't messing with that thread.

His priority was to do what he must to keep her safe.

And suddenly he was enveloped by a waft of memory. Ten years ago. He and Beth were newly dating, med students together. She was little, feisty, cute. Messy chestnut curls. Big brown eyes. Okay, maybe cute wasn't a good enough description. Gorgeous.

He'd asked her out and couldn't believe it when

she'd said yes—and a month later they'd spent a weekend camping.

A week after that she was in hospital with encephalitis, a mosquito-borne virus.

The day he most remembered was a week after that. She was still in hospital, fretting about missing her next assignment. He'd brought her in chocolates and flowers—corny but it was all he could think of. He was twenty-two years old, a kid, feeling guilty that she was ill.

But she was recovering. She was laughing at one of his idiotic jokes. Opening the chocolates.

And then, suddenly, she was falling back on her pillows.

'I can't… Luc, I feel so dizzy… My eyes…'

It was optical neuritis, a rare but appalling side-effect of encephalitis. It had meant almost instant, total blindness.

For weeks she'd had no sight at all, and his guilt had reached stratospheric proportions.

Beth's parents were…absent, to say the least. Suddenly Beth seemed solely dependent on him.

The next few weeks had been a nightmare, for her and for him. His carefree existence was finished. He'd dated her because she was gorgeous, vivacious, funny. Now she was his responsibility.

Blind and bereft, with no other options, she'd agreed to come home with him. He'd cared for her, protected her...and loved her? He still wasn't sure where care ended and love started but her need filled something inside he hadn't been aware was missing.

Her sight gradually returned, not fully but enough to manage. If she was careful. If she was protected.

And as the months went by their relationship had deepened. She'd lain in his arms and he'd known she felt safe and loved. That felt good enough for him. He'd lost sight of the carefree, bubbly girl he'd dated but in her place he had someone who'd need him for ever.

They'd married. And here she was, half-buried in this mess—with a child who wasn't his.

Was there a husband? Was someone else doing the protecting?

This wasn't the time for questions.

He was pushing memory away, years of training putting him on autopilot. Beth was leaning back, her eyes closed as he inserted an IV line.

'This'll make you sleepy,' he told her. 'Relax into it, sweetheart.'

'Toby...'

'You want us to take Toby? Beth, I swear I'll take care of him.'

'How do I know you mean that?' She even managed a smile. 'Of course you will.'

'How old is he?'

'Twenty months.'

'Is there someone we can call who he'll trust?' Someone to sign papers if he had to be treated? Someone like the baby's father?

She wore no wedding ring. That didn't mean anything. Did it?

And once again his heart did this stupid lurch. This was Beth. His Beth. He wanted to gather her into his arms, hold her, keep her safe...

Which was exactly why she'd walked away from him eight years ago. Into...this.

'Margie,' she managed. 'At the childcare centre. Toby trusts...'

The childcare centre at the plaza? He was pretty sure it had been safely evacuated, but he couldn't be sure of every individual. Right now he could only focus on one trapped woman—a woman who was also his wife.

Ex-wife.

But no matter who she was, she was in trouble and she had no need to be worried by anything else.

Her voice was starting to drag and Luc thought the time for Beth to make decisions was over.

'Right,' he said, firmly and surely. 'Let's get Toby out of here, Beth, so we can concentrate on freeing your leg.'

'You'll look after him? If Margie can't?' Through the haze of pain and drugs, her voice was still fierce. 'Luc, swear?'

'I swear,' he said, and something inside him hurt. Badly. That she could still ask this of him... That she could still trust him...

He'd wanted this, so much, but to happen here, in this way...

And despite the pain and the fear, Beth must have sensed it. Her hand caught his and held.

'Luc, I swore I'd never need you again but I need you now. Thank you...'

His throat was so thick he couldn't speak, and it wasn't from the dust. He squeezed her hand back and then carefully lifted the sleeping child away from her breast. The little boy snuffled against Luc, recoiling a little as his face hit the repellent fabric of Luc's high vis jacket, and then relaxing again as Luc hauled a cloth someone handed him around the little boy's face. Luc tucked it in, giving him a soft place to lay his head as well as protection from the dust.

There were hands willing, wanting to take him, to carry him to safety, and Luc's priority had to be with Beth. But still he took a moment to hold, to feel the child's weight in his arms, to feel the steadiness of his breathing, his sleeping, trusting warmth.

He would take care of him. He'd take care of them both.

He must.

The next hour passed in a blur of medical need. The rest of the team was here now, with Blake in charge. They were panning out through the ruins, removing the need for Luc's attention to be on anything but Beth. Still trapped, she needed constant monitoring.

She was semiconscious, drugged to the point where pain and her surroundings were a haze.

Finally, moving with infinite caution, aware that a break in the concrete over her leg could mean parts of it would topple and cause more damage, the slab was lifted. Finally Beth was extricated.

She'd been wearing pants and leather boots. That had been a blessing—it had stopped lacerations that might well have been serious enough for her to bleed out. There was no doubt there were fractures, but blood still seemed to be getting through. Luc knew the greatest danger was the fact that the leg had been compressed for so long.

He accompanied the stretcher across the debris to the makeshift receiving tent the team had set up.

'Status?' Blake Cooper, ER consultant, had been working on an elderly man as Luc brought Beth in. The sheet drawn up over the man's face told its own story, as did the slump of Blake's shoulders.

'Lacerations, bruises, but priority's a broken ankle and crushed lower leg,' Luc told him.

Blake cast him a fast, concerned look. His voice was thick, Luc realised, and it wasn't from dust. 'Do you need me to assess?' He and Blake had worked together for so long they trusted each other implicitly. Luc knew Blake wasn't asking about Luc's ability, it was all about what he could see in Luc's face.

He shook his head. The stretcher was set down on the examination bench and almost unconsciously Luc's hand slid into Beth's and held it.

Blake saw, and the concern on his face grew, but there was no room for explanation.

Neither was there room for evasion, from Blake or from Beth herself. It would be great to say, *Beth's ankle's broken. We'll fix it in no time*, but the one thing he and Beth always had was total honesty. Sometimes it had broken them in two but it was something he couldn't change. He knew she was listening through her haze of medication. Her medical degree meant she'd recognise sugar coating and he had to say it like it was.

'I've given a peripheral nerve block,' he told Blake. 'There's definitely fracture and disloca-tion of the ankle, and we need to check for compartment syndrome.' Compartment syndrome had to be considered here. It was caused by extended crushing of the lower limb, forcing buildup of pressure in one section and loss of pressure in another. The long-term damage of sustained crushing was...unthinkable.

'Do what you have to do,' Beth said weakly, and Blake looked down into her face.

'Hi,' he said. 'I'm Dr Blake Cooper. You are...'

'This is Beth,' Luc said hoarsely, and then he added, because it seemed absurdly important for Blake to know. 'Blake, Beth's a doctor. She's also...my ex-wife.'

There was a moment's stillness while Blake took that on board. He searched Luc's face and Luc could see him reassemble priorities. And then it was business as usual.

'I'm very pleased to meet you,' Blake said, smiling down at Beth. 'Though I could wish the circumstances were different.' He took her wrist and felt her pulse, his face set in the lines of someone accustomed to triage, priorities. And Luc knew Beth was a priority. The risk of delayed treatment with compartment syndrome meant the possibility of a lifetime of pain, numbness or even amputation.

'We need to get the pressure in your foot checked now,' he said to Beth. 'You know what's going on?'

He'd accepted Beth's medical background without question. 'I... Yes,' Beth managed.

'Okay, I'm taking over,' Blake told her, with another fast glance at Luc. And Luc knew the glance. It was an order.

Step away, Luc. You're now a relative, too close to be objective and you need to let me take things from here.

'Beth, we need Luc on triage,' he told Beth. 'You know there's a small hospital here? I'm taking you through into Theatre. If I think there's pressure differential—and by the look of it I suspect that's inevitable—then I'll make an incision to decompress. Your ankle will need to be stabilised. That can be done in Sydney but the pressure needs to be taken off now. Is that okay with you?'

'I... Fine,' Beth managed. 'But... Toby?'

Blake looked a question at Luc and Luc managed to haul his attention from Beth to answer.

'Toby's Beth's son. Twenty months old. He was brought out half an hour ago.'

Some of the tension on Blake's face eased. 'A toddler. I saw him. Sam did the assessment and he's fine. He woke as she was examining him, demanding someone called Wobit...'

'Robert,' Beth said faintly. 'Rabbit.'

'Hey, we guessed right.' Blake smiled down at her. 'Apparently he was dropped, but one of the paramedics remembered and scooted over and rescued him.'

'We've also found your bag and purse,' Luc told her, still trying to keep his voice steady. 'How good are we? But now... Is there anyone we can call to look after Toby?'

'He has to come with me,' Beth managed. 'If I need to go to Sydney, Toby comes too. Luc, please... I need you to promise... I need...'

And something settled deep within.

'It's okay,' Luc said, and touched her face. 'I'll take care of him. I'll take care of you.'

And she managed a smile.

And then something odd happened. It was almost as if a ghost had touched him on the shoulder. He was looking down into Beth's grimed, dust-caked, filthy face, but all he saw was the smile. And in that smile…strangely this wasn't the Beth he'd remembered for the long years of divorce, the Beth who'd been his wife, the Beth he'd cared for for so long. Despite the filth, the fear, the pain, somehow this was Beth as he'd first seen her—a fellow med student laughing at him over a bench in the pathology lab. Her eyes had been sparkling with mischief. Someone must have made a joke. He couldn't remember what it was now. All he remembered was how he'd been caught in that smile, almost mesmerised.

He'd forgotten, he thought. In all those years of need and care, and then the long separation, he'd forgotten what a beautiful woman she was. Stunning.

How could he be remembering now? What the…?

'I'll take it from here,' Blake told him, looking at him strangely.

'Thanks, Blake.'

He had work to do. He had to leave—but heaven only knew the effort it cost him to move away.

From…his wife?

CHAPTER THREE

THE SURGERY BLAKE performed was primitive and fast, making incisions to equalise pressure and ensure that blood supply wasn't compromised before Beth could safely be transported. But Luc wasn't involved. With Beth in Theatre, with Toby safe, he needed to be back in the plaza.

In a sense they were lucky, Luc thought as he worked on. The injuries stayed within the scope of what he and the team could handle. If there'd been compromised breathing of more than one patient or, as sometimes happened in these appalling situations, the necessity for amputation in order to get people out, Beth's foot would have dropped on the triage list and Blake would have been needed out here in the plaza. But the efforts of Luc and the rest of the team were enough.

Not enough, though, for the five people pronounced dead at the scene, or the pilot of the plane, but Luc had worked in enough disasters to know how to block tragedy and keep going.

But he couldn't block the thought of Beth. The thought of what was happening in Theatre. The vision of her trapped and wounded in the rubble. The feel of her hands clutching her child...*her child*! Had she remarried? Where had she been all these years?

How could he have let her go? There'd seemed no choice—she'd given him no choice—but the rush of memory from that smile was doing his head in. Did some other man have the right to that smile?

He was trying desperately to focus but when he finished treating a teenager with a lacerated arm, he turned and saw Blake and he almost sagged with relief.

'O-okay?' Hell, where was his voice? And what was he doing, asking if she was okay? She was suffering from an injured foot, not anything life-threatening.

'She'll live,' Blake said, surveying him cautiously. Luc was known on the team for staying calm in any situation. He needed to get a grip now. Now!

'I've done what I can,' Blake told him. 'She has a fractured ankle but seemingly no other significant injury. The main problem is crush syndrome—compartmentalising—but I've done what I can to equalise pressure and I'm optimistic. But she needs an orthopod and a decent podiatric surgeon to evaluate muscle injury. We're evacuating her on the next chopper and I'm sending you back, too.'

'If I'm needed…'

Once again he got that careful, appraising look. Blake and Luc swapped in and out of the role of chief medic on site. They were both accustomed to checking team members for stress, and maybe—definitely—Blake could see Luc's stress now.

'We have enough medics on the ground here,' he said now, roughly.

And Luc thought, Dammit, he's worried. About me?

'I've been talking to the local doc. Apparently this town has three doctors. Maryanne Clarkson's in her fifties, solid, unflappable. She's working her butt off in Casualty now. There's been an older doctor called Ron McKenzie, in his seventies, and your Beth. Ron and Beth run a clinic in the plaza, right by the car park. Ron's one of the casualties. Maryanne tells me your Beth's a single mum with no family here. Toby, her son, usually stays in childcare in the centre while she works. That's in the plaza, too. The staff did a magnificent job getting the kids out but they're all traumatised. Maryanne says that means there's no obvious person to care for Toby, and no one's stepped forward to be her accompanying person. So in view of that, I'm electing you. Unless the divorce was so acrimonious...'

'I... No.'

'Then you'll do it? She needs medical care during evacuation. I want blood supply to that foot constantly monitored. And she needs someone she knows.'

'And the child...'

'Does he know you?'

'I... No.' How could he know him? Until two hours ago Luc hadn't known he existed.

'Lucky you're good with kids, then,' Blake told him, moving on. 'I'm sending Beth and a guy with fractured ribs and lacerations. Plus Toby.

There's room on the chopper and he's breathed in enough concrete dust to warrant twenty-four-hour obs. They're in your hands, Luc.'

'Right.'

Of course it was right. How many times had he done this, accompanying injured back to Sydney?

But Beth.

And her son.

She was a single mum? There'd been someone else. Had she walked away from him, too?

There was something inside him that clenched and wouldn't unclench.

He took a deep breath and struggled to focus. He needed to hand over what he'd done.

'Leave it, Luc,' Blake said roughly. 'Sam'll fill me in on what you've been doing. Your head's with Beth. Sorry, mate, but from now on I need to treat you as compromised. Are you sure you can manage on the plane?'

'Of course.'

'There's no of course about it. Where family's concerned…'

'Beth's not my family.'

'No? Well, maybe for now she has to be because, as far as I understand, she doesn't have anyone else. If it was Sam injured…'

Where had that come from? Blake and Sam—Samantha, SDR's newest recruit—had become an item and were now engaged to be married. They were a couple. There was no comparison.

Or maybe there was.

Until death do us part?

He and Beth had signed the divorce papers but those long-ago vows still whispered in his head. Telling him Blake was right.

Beth was injured. She wasn't family—how could she be? But somehow there were ties that meant that, yes, he'd stay beside her. For as long as he was needed.

'Beth?'

She'd been stirring for a while now, struggling to surface from a drug-induced sleep, fighting down fears crowding in from all sides. She'd been vaguely aware of being carried to a helicopter, being lifted aboard. She remembered the surge of fear as she'd thought she was being taken from Toby, but a paramedic had stooped over her stretcher, showing her a warmly wrapped bundle.

'He's asleep, Beth, but he's coming with us.'

'We even have Robert Rabbit, a bit scruffy but safely tucked in with him.' And it was Luc, a growly voice in the background. He'd been supervising the loading of another patient onto the chopper. She remembered thinking that was what Luc did. He got people out of trouble. He cared…

That care had been so stifling it had ended their marriage, but as she'd been lifted onto the chopper she'd sunk into it. She hadn't had a choice. Let Luc care and be grateful for it.

And now… They were in the air and he was saying her name, touching her shoulder. 'Beth? Stop fighting it, love. You're safe. But if you're awake…there's something you might like to see.'

Love? How long since anyone had called her that? But it was wrong. She should…

She couldn't. She let the word wash over her and insensibly it made her feel…okay.

'This is amazing,' Luc was saying. 'Can I help you sit up a little?'

'Wh-what?'

'This is too stunning to miss,' Luc was saying. 'And it might even make you feel better. You're supposed to be strapped in. Derek's right here beside you but he's fast asleep. He's copped broken ribs and lacerations and the morphine has put him out like a light. Toby's asleep, too, but I know you're awake. We have your glasses. As long as we can do this without moving your leg, you're okay to see. Beth, there's a thunderstorm. Let me help you.' And he was right beside her, gently raising her shoulders, cradling her against him, adjusting her glasses on her nose. 'Look out the window.'

She did—and she gasped in wonder.

The drugs she'd been given had taken away all pain. Confusion and fear faded. She felt warm and close to sleep. She was being cradled by… by…

Yeah, that was too hard to think about. She tried to block out the feel of him and focussed instead on what lay out the window.

It was indeed a thunderstorm, a massive one, enveloping Sydney in an awe-inspiring display.

Lightning flashed across the sky in a mass of jagged forks, splitting and splitting again.

The entire sky was lit. The lightning seemed all around them. In the distance she could see the lights of Sydney. The Harbour Bridge. The amazing Opera House. They were lit themselves, but as each crack of lightning sizzled, their lights mingled with what nature was providing.

The drugs were making her fuzzy, weird, stunned. The sky outside was surreal.

Luc was holding her. Luc…

Focus. Lightning. Toby.

Danger? She should…she should…

'You're safe, love,' Luc said again, as if he guessed her fears. Which of course he always had. 'It looks stunning but it's well to the north and moving away. Our heliport's on the roof of Bondi Bayside Hospital. We're giving the storm a few minutes to clear before we land but we'll have you and Toby tucked up and safe in no time.'

So she could relax. She could lie back in his arms and let the wash of what looked like a massive pyrotechnic display stun her into silence. She could look out into the dark, stormy world and know that Luc had her safe.

She mustn't. Once upon a time she'd fallen for

that sweet, all-enveloping trust and it had led to heartache and despair. She had to pull away.

But the drugs wouldn't let her and neither would her will. She'd been alone for so long. The fear of the time spent trapped was still with her. The terror.

Luc had her safe and she couldn't fight. For now...once again she had to let him care.

And then they landed and Luc had to take a step back. Blake had obviously forewarned the admission staff and Luc was greeted with something other than professional efficiency. These people were his friends. A barrage of questions was about to descend on him, but not now. He handed over notes and suddenly he was being treated as a relative. Paediatric staff took over the sleeping Toby's care. The orthopaedic team moved in and Beth was wheeled away to Theatre.

She'd been lucky, Luc thought. Or sort of lucky. Most of the crises his team attended didn't have the luxury of an onsite hospital, but Beth had had excellent treatment before transfer. Blake had been able to stabilise pressure, and she was now in the care of one of the best medical teams in Australia.

Bondi Bayside Hospital. The specialists here were world class.

But for now Luc wasn't one of them. Not that he was one of the permanent staff anyway. His role was that of emergency consultant, but he worked here only between medical crises outside the hospital. He couldn't imagine working in the same place day after day. Standing still. Ceasing to need the adrenaline of rescue.

Putting the past behind him.

The past was with him now. He stood in the admissions centre and stared out into the night. They'd been lucky to land when they had. The break in the rolling storms was over. Rain was battering the wide glass windows in the entrance foyer.

Midnight. The place was almost deserted. Ghost-like.

It was at times like this that the ghost of his past reappeared.

Ellen. Seven years old. Bright, bubbly, joyous. Naughty.

'Take your cousin to the playground, Luc.'

Those words were still seared into his head. He'd been nine years old. His mother and his aunt had been having a beer or three with lunch, and Ellen's chatter had been interfering with their gossip. 'And take care of her. You know she's a bit silly. You're responsible.'

So off they'd gone, the half a block to the playground.

Luc's best friend, Nick, had been there with his mum. Nick's mum had been immersed in a book, happily reading. He remembered feeling pleased to see her.

He remembered feeling safe. It was a feeling he didn't have all that often with his mum. Or his aunt. But Nick's mum was okay.

So Ellen had raced for the swing, while Luc and Nick had headed for the see-saw, seeing who could bang the other hardest against the ground as they rose and fell.

He could still see Nick's face laughing up at him.

Then, out of the edge of his eye, he'd seen the swing, suddenly empty, swinging wildly as Ellen jumped off. Then kids on the other side of the road. With a puppy…

'Hey!' Ellen's childish yell was seared into his memory. 'Candy, wait, it's me, Ellen. Is that your new puppy?'

He didn't have time to react. No one did. Ellen was already halfway across the road.

The car had nowhere to go.

And afterwards… The nightmare of adults, screaming, sobbing. 'Who's supposed to be caring for her? Of all the stupid, criminal…'

Nick's mother. 'She's not mine. I didn't even see…'

Then his mother and aunt, haggard, hysterical, dragged from their beer and pleasure to confront a nightmare. His aunt. 'We told you to take care of her, you stupid, stupid boy.'

His own mother. 'It's my fault, Lucy. I thought he was responsible. I thought I could depend on him.'

'It is his fault.' His aunt had hissed it at her, hissed it at him. 'Get him out of my sight.'

What followed was vitriol, recriminations and consequences. His aunt had kicked them out and the cycle of crises and homelessness had resumed.

Until finally… 'I can't care for both of us.' His

mother, sober for once, flat and inflexible. 'You got us into this mess, Luc. You face the cost.'

The cost was foster care. Loneliness. Knowing it was all his fault.

Somehow he'd fought his way through it. He'd had a couple of decent sets of foster parents. He'd been smart, and study had been a way to block out pain.

He'd made it into medicine. He'd almost felt... in control?

And then he'd met Beth and taken her camping. The virus. Her blindness.

And now this.

He hadn't even been able to protect Beth. His own wife...

He felt like smashing something. Anything.

He was going nuts here. He had to do something.

He still had Beth's holdall, with her day-to-day stuff. Her phone. Toddler gear. A briefcase of patients' notes shoved on top. Her glasses.

She'd need her glasses.

Thankful for a specific task he headed for the admission desk. The receptionist greeted him cautiously. She knew him—of course she did. Gossip would have reached her as fast as the hospital grapevine would allow, which in Luc's experience was pretty much faster than the speed of light.

'You've admitted Beth…'

'Carmichael? You know she's in Theatre?' She paused while she thought about where to take it, and came down on the side of forgetting about the Doctor before his name and treating him as a relative. 'You know, you might like to pop home and take a shower,' she told him, and for the first time Luc realised he was still liberally encrusted with concrete dust. 'We'll ring you the moment she's out.'

'Right,' he growled. 'What ward's she going to?'

'Orthopaedic,' she said, sounding surprised, and then realised what he really wanted. 'Whoops, sorry.' She checked a list on her screen. 'Oh. We're almost full so we've had to pop her into a double. She's in with Harriet. Harriet's going to Rehab in the morning so your Beth will have a great room for the rest of her stay.'

Your Beth?

He didn't want to go there.

Focus on the room. Harriet's room was spacious and the admission staff had tried hard to keep it occupied only by Harriet. It would have been one of the last beds left.

'But she'll go to Recovery first,' the receptionist said helpfully. She gave him her best reassuring smile. 'I'm sure she'll be fine.'

'I'll take her bag up and leave it for her,' he growled, and the receptionist looked surprised. As if she was questioning why Luc was bothering to tell her.

It was no big deal, he thought. He and Beth hadn't been married for eight years now. She was just another patient.

Except she wasn't.

The nurses had been in and prepared Beth's space. All was in readiness. The room was dark, silent. Waiting. Harriet was asleep.

How often during the last few weeks had he popped in to see Harriet during the night? She wasn't coping well with the new norm of a leg that'd always be problematic. The rock fall had almost been lethal. Lightning reflexes had saved

her but she'd been left with a comminuted fracture of her tibula and fibula, and there'd been
significant soft tissue and nerve damage. She'd
come close to losing her leg. Compared to Harriet's injury, Beth's was minor and he knew Harriet spent hours staring at the ceiling, trying to
figure where to take life from here.

So he often came in here and sat, but this
night…it was very, very different.

He should go home and have his shower, he
thought, but instead he left the bag, then headed
for the sluice room, stripped off his filthy outer
gear, washed and then returned to Beth's ward.

Harriet's ward, he reminded himself. After all,
Harriet was his friend. Beth was… Beth was…

He wasn't sure what Beth was. He sat in the
darkened room and waited and tried to settle.

Ha.

His phone vibrated in his pocket and he headed
out into the corridor to answer.

'Dr Braxton?'

'Yes.' It was an internal call and his breath
caught. Beth was in Theatre. What was happening?

'It's Recovery,' the nurse on the other end of

the line told him. 'You're on her form as contact person.'

'Yes. Are things...?' Strange how his mouth was suddenly dry. This was only a fractured leg, he told himself, but still... 'Is everything okay?'

'Beth's waking now. She's asking for you—and for someone called Toby?'

'That's her son.'

'Is he okay?'

'He's fine. He's asleep in kids' ward. Observation only—no obvious injuries.' He'd checked in on the way to Beth's ward. Toby had been bathed and was sleeping with his rabbit.

'She's not really out of it yet,' the nurse was saying. 'But her first words were frantic. I'm wondering...we'll be sending her up to the ward in about half an hour. Would it be possible for her to see her son? I have a feeling she won't settle until she's seen him safe. And you, too.'

'She won't be worried about me.'

'Really?' The nurse sounded dubious. 'She sounded...well, be that as it may, if Toby's okay could you arrange to have him there, just for a moment so she can see for herself?'

'Of course.'

But…

He thought of lifting Toby and carrying him through the darkened rooms to sit with him while he waited for Beth…

It felt like a weird, sweet web was closing about him. A web he'd once embraced and he knew he would again—the web of being needed.

'Luc…'

She was enveloped in darkness, though shimmers of light were breaking through. Harsh light. There was something beeping beside her. Her hand…there was something on her hand.

She was trapped. The fear was like a tidal wave, smothering her to the exclusion of everything else.

'Toby.' She heard her own anguish. 'Toby. Luc…'

'Beth?' It was a nurse, speaking in cool, professional and blessedly grounding tones. 'It's okay. You're safe and so is your son. You've been in surgery for a fractured ankle. It's gone well and now you're in Recovery. You're safe, Luc's safe and so is Toby. I promise.'

The light settled. She opened her eyes and it

really was light, normal light, reassuring light. A nurse was smiling down at her.

Would she ever get over that fear of darkness?

'It's okay,' the nurse said again. 'They tell me you've been in real trouble but you're safe now. We've stabilised your ankle, we've cleaned up your cuts and bruises and you're going to be fine. And I've spoken to your Dr Luc. Your ex-husband, they're telling me? What a dark horse he is, we never knew. I can tell you now, though, whatever's in your past the reason you married him must still hold true. There's no one more caring, and right now he's caring for Toby. They're up in the ward, waiting for you. As soon as the effects of the anaesthetic fade, we'll have you with them. So close your eyes now, Beth, and let us care for you.'

She let the words wash over her for a moment, settle. Luc, caring for Toby. Of course. He would. And because it was Toby she had to be grateful. Again.

She was. But…

'I don't think I will close my eyes,' she whispered. 'I don't want the darkness.'

'There's nothing to be afraid of.'

You have no idea, Beth said to herself as she absorbed the reality of where she was, the technology-filled surroundings of the recovery suite. With Luc…somewhere. You have no idea of how much reason there is to be very afraid.

CHAPTER FOUR

TOBY WOKE BRIEFLY and whimpered as Luc lifted him from his cot. If he'd woken completely and wailed he might have left him where he was, but he was obviously a kid used to a working mum, odd hours, childcare. He didn't panic. The nurses helped Luc wrap him in soft, cuddly blankets. He had his rabbit. He snuggled against Luc's shoulder and he slept again.

Luc carried him back to Beth's ward—Harriet's ward—and settled into a visitor's chair to wait. Toby slept on, peaceful, supremely trustful. Leaving Luc to his thoughts.

And Luc thought of what Beth had been doing. Working as a family doctor? The difficulties she'd be facing would be enormous, he thought, but to do it with a child...

Where was the father? As far as he could figure she was on her own, and if she was... Toby must be used to being shared.

He held him close and he felt…he felt…

'Want to tell me what's going on?'

It was Harriet, speaking sleepily from the bed on the far side of the room. 'Luc? Is that you?'

'It's me,' he growled.

'Are you holding…a baby?'

'Toby.'

'Toby.' She was speaking as if she wasn't sure where she was going. 'It's true, then. One of the nurses said my new roomie is about to be…your ex-wife? She was under the rubble?'

'Beth.' The whole hospital would know by now, he thought grimly. The grapevine would be in overdrive.

'Beth?' Harriet was suddenly wide awake. They'd both kept their voices low in deference to the sleeping Toby. The lights were dim. It was a weirdly intimate setting. A place for asking… and telling…secrets? 'Is she okay?'

'Lacerations, bruises, plus a broken ankle. She was trapped by falling concrete so compartment syndrome was an issue, but she's had excellent, fast treatment. She's in Recovery now and the surgery's gone well.'

'That's great.' But Harriet's voice still sounded cautious. 'The baby...'

'He's twenty months.'

'Toddler, then. Is he yours?'

And that was a stab from left field. It was a question that required a simple no, but as he held the little boy close there were so many mixed feelings...

Is he yours?

He wasn't. He wasn't anything to do with him. So why did he feel...?

'No,' he managed. 'We've been apart for eight years.'

'Want to tell Aunty Harry about it?'

'I... No.'

'Hey, that's hardly reasonable. How much have I told you about me?'

And he had to concede that was fair.

He and Harriet had worked side by side in situations that'd be enough to give normal people nightmares. They'd become the best of friends. Once upon a time he'd even asked her out and her response still made him smile. 'What? Us? It'd be like dating my twin.'

It was true. Over the years, in the waiting

times between crises, evacuating patients to-gether, depending on each other's skills, they'd become a team, but it wasn't until these last few weeks that Harriet had talked about her past. And now... It was his turn?

'So you've been married?'

'I told you.'

'And your ex-wife is about to share my ward. Is she a monster?'

'No!' Unconsciously he held Toby a little closer. 'She's...an amazing woman.'

'The nurses are saying she's a doctor.'

'Yes.'

'And you split when?'

'I... Eight years ago.'

'So Toby?'

'I have no idea who Toby's father is. No one at the scene seemed to know. They're saying she's a single mum. That's why we brought him with us.'

'And it's why the admin staff listed you as next of kin. The nurses told me. Honestly, this is all over the hospital. Luc Braxton's secret love child. Or not.' She was eyeing him cautiously and Luc thought she was using him to take her mind off her own troubles. So when she pushed further… 'Come on, Luc, tell all,' he finally did.

'Beth and I dated at med school,' he told her. 'And then she copped encephalitis, with complications. Optical neuritis. For months she was almost completely blind. She regained some sight but it's still…not perfect. Not even close. We married and I took care of her, but…she hated it. And it was more than hating the disability. She hated…having to depend on me. I didn't mind— hell, it was me who took her camping. I probably caused the damned mosquito bite, but she fought me every inch of the way. How many times she burned herself, hurt herself because she wouldn't let me help. And then she swore she'd finish medicine. I thought…maybe with help she could get through. She could think about something like psychiatry but she wouldn't accept her limitations. And now…hell, Harry, she's been practising as a family doctor. Plus she's got a kid. What's she been thinking?'

'Wow,' Harriet said softly. 'She sounds like some woman.'

'She's an independent, stubborn, foolhardy…'

'Yeah, just like me saying I want to go back to Specialist Disaster Response.'

'It's not the same.'

'No? But then you have a warped view on what you'd do yourself compared to what you expect the rest of the world to do.'

'Harry…'

'Hey, I think I'm going to enjoy meeting your Beth,' Harriet said, for once sounding almost cheerful. 'We sound like we'll get along. Common enemy and all that. Speaking of which, isn't that the sound of the theatre lift arriving? Pull my curtains, Luc. I'll try for sleep and leave you to your Beth.'

'One, two, three, lift…'

How many times had she heard that, the phrase used by every paramedic as they shifted patient from trolley to bed, from bed to trolley?

She'd never heard it referring to her, though. Even when the encephalitis had been at its worst, she'd been able to move herself. She could help.

Even if Luke hadn't wanted her to.

'Be careful.'

And the words from beside her slammed her

back to a time past, the warning, the voice, the care that seemed to be swinging its way through the fog of this nightmare night. It was Luc's voice. *Be careful?* She held the thought. How could she not be careful when that voice was with her?

'She's in safe hands.' It was an older, big-bosomed woman, talking as the nurses plumped pillows under her head and tucked warmed blankets around her. Beth could hear the smile in the woman's voice. 'I'm Hilda Heinz, orthopaedic surgeon,' she told Beth. 'I should have caught up with you in Recovery but we've had a queue. No matter. We've done a lovely job on your ankle. It's beautifully aligned and should heal really well. The team on site did a great job preventing long-term damage through crush injury and I envisage a good recovery. A few days in here until the swelling subsides, a sexy black boot, compliance with rules, a spot of rehab and you'll be as good as new by Christmas.'

By Christmas… Three months…

'But not to worry about that now,' Hilda was saying. 'All you need to know is that you're fine. Your surgery's all done and here's Dr Braxton holding your little boy. Sound asleep. Oh, what a sweetheart. No, don't you move. Any pain? No? Excellent. If you have any breakthrough push this button here, PCA—patient-controlled analgesia—you know how it works? Great. The buzzer's right by your other hand. Dr Braxton, let us know when you leave, and the nurses will take over obs from then.'

And she whisked away with the nurses, and Beth was left lying in the dim light, trying to regain her bearings.

Which seemed very shaky indeed.

'Toby…' That seemed important to say, and Luc gently lifted his bundle across so she was within inches of her little boy's face.

He was still sleeping.

Toby was a doctor's kid, used to being cared for by others, used to being lifted in the dead of night when she finally finished at the hospital and carried him home.

When she'd first moved to Namborra it had seemed more than enough that she was finally able to practise medicine. But then, settled, working hard, living within the community, she'd allowed herself to think past her career.

Another relationship seemed impossible. After Luc…well, she wasn't going there again. But a baby…

And one night she'd talked about it to the elderly doctor she worked with. She'd just given Ron a sky-dive for his seventieth birthday. He was lit from within. After years of struggling with the death of his wife, treating himself as old and useless, he was back in partnership with her. They both had issues, but between them they reckoned they made one and a half very competent doctors. After the sky-dive Ron was ready to declare the one and a half description was an underestimation.

'There's nothing we can't do,' he'd declared. 'So, Beth, why don't you have a baby? Use donor semen—whatever? And don't say you can't do it alone. You know this whole town will help you.'

They could. They did, which was why Toby was accustomed to sleeping in strangers' arms. Which was why Luc could hold him and he didn't stir.

Luc… It was eight years since she'd seen him.

He was a stranger.

Focus on Toby.

She wasn't wearing her glasses, but they wouldn't help much in dim light anyway. So she did as she so often did. She saw through touch.

She put her hand out and drew her baby's face, reassuring herself there were no scratches. No tears. His eyes were closed. His little mouth was still...perfection.

'The rest of him's great, too,' Luc said gently as her palm cupped his cheek. 'The paediatric staff have gone all over him. He's perfect.'

Why did that make her want to cry?

Why did Luc's voice make her want to cry?

She had an almost irresistible urge to move her hand from Toby's face to Luc's, to let herself feel what was the same, what was different.

So much was different. She was different. She'd fought for her independence and won, but at what cost?

'Hey,' he said softly as she closed her eyes and stopped trying to see. 'Welcome back to the land of the un-squashed, Dr Carmichael. I can't tell how good it feels to see you on this side of the slab of concrete.'

She thought about that for a while, and the warmth, the doziness from the drugs, the knowledge that Toby was safe—and, yes, the fact that Luc was beside her—faded into the background as memories from the afternoon flooded back. The noise. The fear...

'What happened?' she managed. 'I mean...it was a plane?'

'A cargo plane,' he told her. 'Best guess at the moment is that the pilot had some sort of collapse—maybe an infarct. He ploughed along the top of the plaza, bringing the roof down. The concrete pillars supporting the undercover car park folded—that was where you were. The plane then crashed into the sports oval. No one was on the oval.'

She thought about that for a while. She tried to feel relief, but...

'The pilot?'

'Killed instantly, but maybe he was dead beforehand. That's up to the coroner to decide.'

'And...' How hard was it to ask? 'The plaza? The...the childcare centre?'

'Lots of noise and dust and frightened children. They were trapped for a while but the staff had the sense not to try and shift things to get them out. They're all safe.'

'There's more, though,' she whispered, remembering the crash, the screams, the terror. 'I know…'

'There is.' She could hear the reluctance in his voice and she knew he'd tell her. When had Luc been anything but honest? 'The car park was the worst hit. We're confirming identities now but the locals were sure even before I got on the chopper with you. As far as we know there were five deaths. Bill Mickle. You know him? The local greyhound trainer? Ray and Daphne Oddie. Farmers in their seventies. A woman called Mariette Goldsworthy, a friend of Ray and Daphne's from out of town. And Ron. Ron McKenzie.' His voice grew even more gentle. 'Ron was killed instantly as he walked down into the car park. They tell me you knew him very well. Another doctor. Your partner? Your friend.'

'Ron…' The distress she felt was almost overwhelming.

'I'm so sorry.' Almost unconsciously his hand slipped into hers and held.

She should pull away. She should…

She didn't. He was cradling her son against his

chest. He was holding her hand. With the little boy between them they made an island of refuge with the baby enclosed, a nucleus of safety and comfort. It was an illusion—she knew it was— but right now she needed it. Soon she'd have to pull away, as she'd pulled away before, but right now her need was too great. Ron…dead. Her best friend.

She held on for all she was worth.

'You should sleep.' He said it softly but he didn't move and she made no effort to let him go. To let the darkness of the night take over.

The memories were suddenly all around her, that night in hospital so long ago when her world had suddenly grown dark. When Luc had seemed all that lay between her and horror.

'Where's your family?' he'd asked then. They'd known each other for such a short time, he hadn't even known.

'Absent,' she'd told him, shortly. They were always absent. Her clever parents, super smart. When the gravity of her illness had become obvious, when she'd been unable to see at all, her father had phoned from Zurich, barking instructions to the medical staff, offering to fly her to the States for some super treatment a colleague was researching. Her mother had flown in from Glasgow and spent two days with her, most of which had been spent on the phone, reorganising commitments. Both of them had transferred money.

'You'll need carers, at least for the short term, and if things don't improve you'll need specialist accommodation. Your father and I will both contribute...'

But Luc had said no such thing. When the time had come for discharge he'd simply picked her up and carried her home. He'd put his studies on hold for six months. He'd cared for her. He'd told her he loved her.

She remembered the first time he'd said it. 'I love you.' Three little words. Her mother signed off emails with the love word all the time.

Love you, sweetheart. Mum.

Apart from that... She couldn't remember anyone using the words. We're proud of you. That was her parents' equivalent. They were proud that she was independent, that when she'd been packed off to boarding school aged five she'd coped. They loved that she didn't need them.

But Luc... The first time she'd met him her heart had done a crazy backflip with pike, and that feeling had never faded. During that short camping trip she'd kept asking herself, could love happen so fast? And then, when she'd been so ill, he'd never once thought of walking away. He'd held her and he'd loved her and she'd thought he'd be her home for ever. For the first time in her life she'd felt cared for, cherished, safe.

But in the end...it was a sweet, sticky mesh, a trap for someone who'd never had such caring, who hadn't realised...what went with it.

But she knew now. Basing marriage—basing *love*—on need led to disaster. It was a lesson hard learned, but by now it was instilled into her bones. So now she found the courage to tug back. He let her go without a protest and she slipped her hand under the covers, as if it could betray her if she didn't hold it close.

'Can you sleep?' he asked.

'I don't...think so.' She felt tears slipping down her face. Ron...

'Want to tell me about Ron?' he asked, and she knew he was giving her space. That was the thing about Luc. He always knew…

'He's…he was amazing.' She forced herself to focus on her friend. His loss was a gut-wrenching emptiness that'd take time to come to terms with—would she ever?—but for now…for now she accepted the invitation to talk about him. It helped. For Ron's sake?

For hers. It stopped…the other ache. The need for her betraying hand to slip from the covers and take Luc's again.

'I met him five years ago,' she whispered, trying to block out Luc's presence and let herself drift without pain. 'After you…after we split I took a job in Brisbane, with their palliative care unit. My sight was slowly improving but there were still restrictions. I worked with a great specialist staff who used me to the maximum but of course there were things I couldn't do. I was desperate to work in family medicine but it seemed I couldn't. And then there was Ron…'

'Tell me.'

'Ron's wife was a hospice inpatient for about four months. She had bone metastases with spinal collapse and needed round-the-clock specialist nursing. Ron was a family doctor but he was almost seventy. He'd been off work for two years as he cared for Claire and when she died he was…bereft. Stranded. He felt old and useless. After Claire's funeral I found the ad for a doctor at Namborra in the medical journal. It seemed a decent medical centre but remote. Desperate for doctors. Ron loved the country. He and Claire had been aching for a country retirement when she fell ill and he was desperate for something, anything to fill the void. So I pointed it out to him and he said: "I will if you will".'

'I don't get it. Weren't you happy in the hospice?'

'Safe, you mean.' It was impossible to keep the old bitterness from her voice. Even now. 'Yes, I was. I was needed. I was used mostly for counselling, for explaining treatments, outcomes, and I could have stayed there for ever. But that's not what I trained to do. I wanted family medicine and Ron gave me that.'

'I don't understand.'

'We offered Namborra one and a half doctors. Ron was slowing down—he had arthritis and a gammy knee. My sight's a problem but the medical board were satisfied that I had enough to get by. With help. So we made the agreement to run clinics together. Patients coming in get sighted by Ron—more and more it's simply Ron doing a quick visual as he calls his own patients. Anyone looking unexpectedly pasty or rashy he tells me, and if anything needs detailed examination I call him. But I have a magnifying head lamp. I can see for injections and IVs—with the magnifying lamp I'm better than someone with fifty fifty vision. The more I know the community the easier it is, and anything needing young and fit, I'm your man. I've even been known to crawl into a car wreck, with Ron backing me on the sidelines. He trusts… He…trusted…'

But then her voice broke. She couldn't go on.

'Sweetheart, enough.' He ran his fingers gently through her hair, something he'd done long ago. She could feel the mat of concrete dust between his fingers and her scalp and she minded. She wanted those fingers closer. 'Enough,' he said again. 'Grieve for Ron tomorrow. For now you need to sleep. You need to take care of you.'

The feel of his fingers, the feeling in her fuzzy mind, was insidious in its sweetness. She could close her eyes and let go. Relax into his caring. But...

'But Toby...' She forced her mind to think. Toby was still cradled against Luc's chest. 'What...what happens to Toby?'

Would he stay in hospital? Would someone call social services?

'Where's his dad?' Luc asked.

'Not on the scene.' Her mind was doing a stupid, scared spiral. She should have insisted he stay in Namborra. She had friends there. Oh, but to leave him...

'Where are your parents?'

'I have no idea.' It didn't matter. Not in a million years would they drop everything to care for their grandson. They'd thought she was insane when she'd told them she was pregnant. 'I guess...if he can stay in hospital tonight...'

But she hated that, too. He'd have scratches—he must have—and the one thing hospitals worldwide had no answer for was the risk of superbugs. It was a small risk but, oh...

Social services, then? Foster care?

The thought was enough to overwhelm her. She felt sick, so nauseous she felt close to vomiting.

But Luc's hand was on hers again, his grip firm.

'It's okay, Beth. If you agree... I'm due for leave. The service hates it accruing, so there's pressure to take it and I'm thinking this is the time I can. I have an apartment just over the road from the hospital. If you agree, I can hit the paediatric staff for a crib, high chair, stroller, bottles, whatever I need. Then I can take him home with me.'

'With you.' The drugs were really kicking in now. She'd had a jab of pain from her foot and had squeezed the morphine feed. Now she wished she hadn't. The night was hazy enough already.

She couldn't see Luc's face. The light was so dim, even if she had normal sight she might not be able to see it.

She remembered all that time ago, when the darkness had closed in. She remembered Luc letting her—encouraging her—to read his face. To run her fingers over the strong bone structure. To let her fingers see his thick, dark hair, the harsh outline of his jaw, the deep set eyes she knew were almost black, the stubble of after-five shadow that seemed to return about two minutes after he shaved. She wanted that now—but surely it was the drugs. It had to be the drugs.

Luc. Taking Toby home with him.

The same sweet trap…

What option did she have? But her night was spinning.

'Hey, you can trust him.' It was a woman's voice from the other side of the curtain. 'Luc, we need an introduction.'

'Harriet,' Luc said, and rose with his sleeping bundle and drew back the curtain. 'Didn't you promise to go to sleep?'

'I said I'd try, not that I would.' In the dim light Beth could make out a figure in the next bed, a woman, with her leg in some sort of traction. 'Hi, Beth,' the woman said. 'You're doing pretty well for post op, post trauma. I'm your roomie, Harriet. I'm also one of Luc's colleagues, part of the SDR service, and just in case you're lying there wondering whether you can trust this guy with your baby, I'm here to tell you he's good.'

'Luc's good?' She was struggling to make her voice work. Oh, her head hurt.

'Hey, Beth, it's time to let go.' Harriet's voice gentled as she heard Beth's confusion. 'You've had one hell of a day. But before you do... Beth, last year your Luc was caught up in a flood rescue. A pregnant mum with three kids. The mum had gone into labour, which was why she'd been too scared to evacuate. She'd been waiting for an ambulance or for her husband to reach her when the water hit. Luc was lowered into the house just on dark. They were surrounded by floodwater and it was too wild to get anyone else down there. So they were stuck there until midmorning. At dawn we went in and found them.

'S-safe?'

'Of course safe,' Harriet said, as if there could never have been any doubt. 'They were stuck in the attic but Mum had delivered her baby safely and Luc had everything under control. Mum was snuggled in bedding Luc had dragged from downstairs. She was warm, safe, cuddling her newborn and the rest of the kids were pretending to be the Lilliputians in *Gulliver's Travels*, using the ropes Luc had used descending to tie him up. I don't know who was having more fun, Luc or the kids. Luc had managed to take diapers, wipes, food, everything they needed, upstairs before the flood destroyed everything in the kitchen, and the kids were gutted they were being rescued. So I'm just saying... Beth, you can trust this guy. Let him take care of your baby and go to sleep.'

What was there in that statement that made Beth weep? There was a stupid tear sliding down her nose and when Luc stooped to wipe it away, she couldn't stop. More followed.

And Luc swore.

'Dammit, Beth, you're past exhausted. But you're safe now, and so's Toby. So, please, trust me. Believe Harriet. You know I can cope. Let me care for you both. Go to sleep.'

Let me care...

How hard had it been eight years ago to walk away from that statement? How much pain had that caused? Yet here it was again, a siren song, and she had no strength to resist.

'Let it go,' he told her, and she had no choice.

'Just...just for tonight,' she managed, and he wiped her face again.

'Of course just for tonight. Worry about tomorrow tomorrow. Sleep now, Beth, and trust me.'

She had no choice. She closed her eyes and let herself sink into something she'd sworn never to need again.

Luc.

He'd just offered to take care of a toddler—for how long? By himself?

Was he out of his mind?

But the thought of not offering almost killed him. How could he not?

Here it comes again, he thought savagely. The need to care. The almost overwhelming urge to take on the safety of the whole world.

He'd even talked to the psych about it.

'Luc, do you think every catastrophe in the world is your fault?'

She'd asked that and he'd grinned and pushed it aside but her question hadn't been a joke.

He thought of the squeal of brakes, his little cousin's body lying on the road, the ring of adults screaming, sobbing, his aunt turning to shake him until his head was almost shaken from his shoulders.

Then Beth…lying terrified in her hospital bed, seeing nothing but darkness. The neuro-surgeon… 'Encephalitis… It's a rare disease and optical neuritis an even rarer complication, but the mosquitoes this year are almost plague pro-portion. Didn't either of you have the sense to use repellent?'

His fault.

He had a twenty-month-old baby boy in his arms. He needed to keep him safe.

Another vision…

Beth, her sight recovering, standing in the lit-tle kitchenette they'd shared. Her finger sticky with blood after a knife had slipped. She'd been chopping carrots.

'So what?' Her reaction had been loaded with frustration, fury. 'You know my sight's return-ing. Do you think I'll let you chop my carrots for ever? Everyone has accidents in the kitchen, Luc.'

'You know your sight's not perfect. I can—'

'No, *I can*.' She'd yelled it at him. 'I can and I will. And, sure, I'll mess up along the way but that's the way it is. No, I'm not perfect but who is? I need to take the odd risk. I need to live, Luc, and I can't do it wrapped in cotton wool.'

'I'm only saying it's sensible to let me—'

'I don't want to be sensible.' She'd sighed and swiped a tissue and wrapped her bleeding finger. 'Enough. This isn't ever going to work. I'm leaving. You get to chop your own carrots. I'm off to chop mine, regardless of whatever blood I shed along the way. You've been fantastic, Luc, but your job is done. You've saved me enough. Now it's time for me to save myself.'

But she hadn't been able to. The memory of her crushed under the rubble was doing his head in.

At least she was being sensible now. She knew she had no choice. She was accepting his caring, which meant… He had sole care of the toddler sleeping solidly in his arms.

A toddler. Help.

As if on cue, Toby stirred and whimpered, and Luc's arms tightened around him. Beth's baby.

He should be…

No, that was an almost creepy thing to think.

Their marriage was years dead. This was his friend's baby, nothing more.

But still he held, and something about the warmth of the little body, the way the toddler curved into him… Something settled inside him.

It felt right to be caring for him. It felt good to be allowed to help.

Years of crisis intervention had involved years of panicked kids. He was known in the team as the kiddie whisperer, with an innate ability to calm panicked kids. He murmured to Toby and held him closer as he headed to kids' ward. What he needed was equipment. There were all sorts of very capable nurses down there to give him all the advice he needed. He could do this.

For however long it took?

He had no choice. This was for Beth. His ex-wife.

Yeah. The only thing was… Why did it feel wrong to put the ex in front of her title?

CHAPTER FIVE

A WEEK LATER Beth was discharged.

Home?

That was a joke, Beth thought as Luc pushed her wheelchair through the hospital entrance into the sunshine. He paused for a moment as though he understood the sheer sensuous joy of emerging from an air-conditioned hospital into… Bondi Beach.

This wasn't home but it felt amazing.

The hospital was built on a rise overlooking the bay. Her hospital room had had views back over the city, but the street from the hospital entrance ran straight down to the sea.

In the week since her accident the Namborra optometrist had sent her a pair of unscratched glasses, plus a year's supply of contact lenses— *Free of charge, Beth, get well fast!* Now the ocean glimmered, sparkled, sang in the morning light and she had an almost overwhelming urge to ditch her wheelchair and jump straight in.

Sadly, her leg was in a giant moon boot, propped on a frame in front of her. She had crutches but Hilda's advice was to use the wheelchair as much as she could.

Toby was sitting happily on her knee, crowing with glee as they emerged into the sunlight, enjoying this amazing new version of a stroller. Luc was behind her wheelchair. Dictating where she went?

That was hardly fair, she reminded herself. He was being extraordinarily generous. For the last week he'd devoted himself to Toby, bringing him in to visit her two or three times a day, showing enormous patience as his life had been taken over by a toddler.

She'd accepted his offer of help, but her choices had been…well, non-existent. She accepted Luc's help or she handed Toby over to welfare.

And now she was becoming even more indebted. Yes, she was being discharged from hospital but she still needed ongoing rehab. That wasn't available in Namborra.

She could have hired herself a furnished apartment but that left her depending on taxis, on outside help. Toby was fast, beetling around his world with toddler disregard for safety. She saw herself launching across strange rooms to prevent catastrophe—with her leg in a massive boot—and knew she had to accept Luc's offer.

'Home straight away?' He must have sensed her need to take deep breaths of the sea air, to gaze out over the ocean, to let herself come to grips with the fact that she was out of hospital, she was healing, she was safe.

As long as she let Luc take control.

'I… What do you mean?'

'I mean I took your gear over to the apartment earlier. We can go straight there now or we could go down to the beach first. It's a great morning.

'You should be at work.'

'I told you, Beth,' he said gently. 'I'm on compulsory holidays.'

'It's not much of a holiday, taking care of us.'

'It's my privilege. I owe—'

'Don't you dare.' Her anger flashed from nowhere. 'You owe me nothing. I went camping with you and a mosquito bit me. We were having a gorgeous time until then, but ever since, every time you look at me all you see is guilt.'

'That's not true.'

'It is,' she said grimly. 'Luc, you know I fell in lust with you the first time I saw you, and that camping trip…wow. Then afterwards, you were so wonderful I didn't see what was under it. That you needed to be needed. All I knew was that I loved being cared for. I loved being cherished. But in the end it almost killed you to let me do something as simple as chop carrots. Luc, we married for all the wrong reasons and I've more than proved I can handle my life alone.'

'But you're injured now.'

'You're telling me that's your fault as well?'

'If you weren't sight impaired…'

'Right, so that concrete pillar wouldn't have fallen on me if I'd been able to look up and see it fall?' She was trying very hard not to twist and yell. 'Oh, for heaven's sake… Luke, it happened in an instant and no one else injured or killed was sight impaired. And the sight thing… Sure, I have trouble in low light. Yes, I need correction, but technology's so great that now…guess what? I can even chop carrots all by myself. I've been doing it for eight years now and I still have every one of my fingers. As soon as I get this stupid boot off my leg I'll be independent again.'

'But you need me now.'

'I do,' she said through gritted teeth. 'But you know what? I intend to treat you like a friend. And the thing with real friends is that they don't need to be thanked all the time, and they'll also accept when to back off. So back off, Luc. Know that I'm incredibly grateful for what you're doing for me, but for the rest... Let me do what I'm capable of, and accept that where I am is nothing to do with you. I have enough to worry about without accepting your guilt. If you can't manage that then I can organise my own apartment and hire babysitters at need.'

'Don't you dare.'

'That's just the problem, Luc. You never let me dare anything.' She glared up at him and then shrugged. 'Okay. I'm grateful. Really I am. Let's go to the beach and forget it.'

And she put her hands on the wheels and shoved, moving the chair forward.

There was a road. A kerb. A drop. A lurch.

She had to let go of the wheels and grab Toby.

Luc caught her before she tilted and fell.

There was a moment's silence while traffic whizzed past. She sat and stared ahead, counting to ten. Then to twenty. She thought about counting to a hundred.

And finally Luc spoke. 'Beth, really, how much can you see?'

Her anger was still with her, but she'd just given herself a fright. She'd shoved her chair toward the road. Toby was on her knee.

She hadn't been totally stupid. Even if she'd fallen she would have just fallen on the kerb. A bike lane protected her from oncoming cars, but still...she had been dumb.

One of the things she'd found hardest, still found hard, was accepting her limitations. She took a deep breath, fought for calm, and finally she said it like it was.

'I'm sorry I scared you,' she managed. 'That was stupid. I need to figure this chair out, what I can and can't do, but what I just did had nothing to do with impaired sight. It was temper. My visual impairment is six/sixty without glasses, but my field of vision is around a hundred and twenty degrees. So, yes, I'm impaired but with my glasses or contact lenses I'm close to normal. Not in dull light, though—being honest, that screws me. Colours fade. Under the concrete… that was terrifying. But that's it, Luc. Usually I can do and see almost everything a normal person can.

'What I did was dumb but here's the thing. I'm not all about my disability. I have hormonal flushes, I have temper, I have impatience, I have all the things normal people have. Because I am normal, Luc. Now I have a broken leg, a guilty conscience and an almost overwhelming urge to get down to the beach. As I'm sure Toby does. Don't you, Toby?'

All this while Toby had been sitting on her knee, beaming at the outside sights, delighted with the fact that he was with his mum, on a wheelchair, an amazing wheeled contraption he'd never seen before. There was enough going on around them to hold his attention. Now, though, she'd said the magic word. His little face turned toward the sea.

'Beach,' he said solidly. And then… 'Spade.'

'Spade?' Beth asked, thrown off track.

'During this last week,' Luc said, almost apologetically, 'Toby and I have been learning to dig. We're not quite down to China but we're close.'

And that took her aback, too. All this week while she'd been struggling with tests, procedures, a mild infection, pain and boredom, Luc had been playing with her son. Playing. She had no doubt of it. Toby had had enough carers in his short life for her to assess how he reacted to them, whether they were full of warmth and fun or whether they treated him as a job.

Whenever Luc had brought him into her room he'd crowed with joy to see her, but the protests when he'd left had been minimal. Sometimes even non-existent. He'd snuggled into Luc as if Luc had known him all his life.

Because they'd dug holes almost all the way to China?

And what was there in that that sent a wash of desolation over her, a wash so great she felt her world was shifting?

It was dumb, she thought. It was because she'd just been released from hospital. Patients often

said release meant a weird feeling of discombob-
ulation, emerging to a world that didn't seem to
have noticed that they'd stepped out for a while.

And while she'd stepped out... Luc and Toby
had formed their own little relationship, and she
hadn't been part of it.

She had to accept the new norm and move on.
She had to step right back onto this spinning
world and be a part of it.

'I would very much like to see you dig a hole
to China,' she managed, with forced cheeriness,
and Luc sent her a sharp look.

'Are you okay? Pain?'

'Leave it, Luc.' She took a deep breath, pushing away the almost dizzy sense of disorienta-
tion. 'No pain. I'm just a bit...befuddled with
everything that's happened. I'm sure what I need
is sand, sun and maybe even an ice cream. If you
could manage that I'd be grateful.'

'But you don't want to be grateful.'

He said it like he was struggling to understand,
and she thought, I'm hurting him. Again.

'No one wants to be grateful,' she managed.
'Giving should be two ways, and for me, the balance has always been a bit lopsided for comfort.

But that doesn't mean I don't love what you're doing for us. Tell you what. You push us down to the beach and I'll buy the ice creams. Deal?'

And he gave her a look she couldn't begin to understand. A look that said even this tiny thing, letting her pay for ice creams, was hard.

That was dumb. They both knew it was dumb and finally he smiled.

'Deal,' he said. 'Can I have a double cone, chocolate on one side, liquorice on the other?'

'Liquorice? What sort of ice-cream freak are you?'

'A man of taste,' he told her. 'What's your poison?'

'Salted caramel every time. And Toby loves rainbow.'

'Rainbow!' He looked appalled. 'Doesn't that make…?'

'An appalling mess? Yes, it does. And you know what? Sight impairment works just fine for that. All I need to do is remove my glasses and my little boy is just a sticky, Technicolor bundle of happiness. You have a problem?'

'I… Not at all.'

'Then let's go,' she said happily. 'We have work to do if we're to reach China by lunchtime.'

Luc parked the wheelchair on the promenade and, despite Beth's protests, lifted her into his arms and carried her toward the shoreline. The sunshine was glorious. Tiny waves ran in and out. The shallow water made a magical play-ground for Toby, and a host of tiny sandpipers had obviously agreed to share.

As Luc carried Beth, Toby staggered along by his side, seemingly entranced that it was his mother being carried and not him. He was equally entranced by the sand between his toes so it meant a long carry—which was fine by Luc.

He was holding Beth in his arms and he'd for-gotten...how right she felt?

She was holding herself stiffly, though, as if she was afraid to relax. The thought was unset-tling. What had he done to make her afraid?

He'd cared. Too much?

How could he limit caring?

He had to, though, or she'd run. He knew it. For all she needed his help, she'd set up boundaries that he couldn't cross. Her body didn't mould against his as it once had. She'd lost...trust.

She'd told him so little of her life for the last eight years. Hell, he didn't even know who Toby's father was, and some gut instinct told him not to ask. She was holding herself tightly contained.

When he set her down by the water's edge she almost visibly relaxed.

'Sunscreen first,' he said, tugging a bottle from his back pocket. And then ice creams.'

'Ice creams when we've done enough to deserve them,' she retorted. 'But hooray for remembering sunscreen. I don't suppose you brought three spades?'

'Two,' he told her. And then at the look on her face he did a fast change of tack. 'My mistake. They sell them at the kiosk. Three bucks fifty each, blue, pink or yellow or red. Toby's is yellow. Mine's blue. Do you have a preference?'

'Pink, of course,' she said happily, and took five dollars out of her purse and handed it over.

He managed to take it. This was a whole new ballgame, he thought as he headed across to the kiosk, and he needed to learn the rules.

When he returned, the hole had been started. Beth and Toby were digging fiercely, a spade apiece.

'Here's yours,' he said, offering her a pink spade with silver sparkles embedded in the plastic handle. 'Plus the change.'

'I've decided I like the blue one,' she said blithely. 'There's been a coup in your absence. Consider the dollar fifty change compensation for the new order. You're in charge of pink and glitter.'

And she chuckled.

It was a good sound. A great sound.

It was a sound that did something inside him he couldn't understand.

But now wasn't the time for asking questions. Toby was digging with fierce concentration, spraying sand as he went. 'Dig,' he said imperatively, and they all dug—and ducked from Toby's sand—and kept right on digging.

Luc got creative. He extended the hole from where they'd started, down to the reaches of the tide. He dug deep so as the tide started to come in, the water rushed in and out of their hole, making Toby squeal with joy. They dug until the hole was big enough for a toddler to sit in and that was a moment of supreme satisfaction.

And that took Beth aback as well, because Toby started tugging his T-shirt and saying— very firmly, 'In!'. Luc emptied the daypack Beth hadn't even noticed until now, producing towel, spare clothes, spare nappy...

'Wow,' Beth breathed. 'If you ever give up medicine can you come back as a childminder? Dibs I have first chance at employing you.'

'Consider me employed,' he said grandly. 'I have more leave due and it would be my very great pleasure to be your childminder.'

Which silenced her.

They'd been divorced for eight years. After all this time...

'Luc, why?' she managed as he expertly stripped her small son and started massaging in more sun lotion. By the way Toby submitted she knew this had been a daily ritual while she'd been hospitalised.

This man had put his life on hold.

'Because we're friends,' he said solidly, and she thought he always had sensed what she was thinking. He was wearing shorts and a T-shirt that stretched a bit tight across his abs. His dark hair looked a bit…messy. He rose and looked down at her, smiling that lopsided sexy smile that had made her fall in love ten years ago and that was doing exactly the same thing now.

Except she wasn't a dumb kid, thrown by accident and disability into falling back into a failed relationship for all the wrong reasons. She was sensible. A mother, a family doctor, a woman who had her own independent future mapped out in front of her. Sort of.

She didn't need to be looking at…abs?

'With no strings,' she managed, and it sounded ungrateful. Or scared. She wasn't sure which but there didn't seem anything she could do about it.

'No strings,' he agreed gravely. 'Just friends, Beth.'

'I… It might be a good time for an ice cream.' She had to break the moment. The way he was looking at her…

The way he was looking…

Toby was done. He was now wearing a swim nappy and nothing else except sun screen. He wriggled out of Luc's grasp and slid into their hole with a resounding splash. An incoming wave filled the hole with foam, and he patted the water with gusto, sending splashes over his mother. He crowed with glee and then caught onto the only word in the preceding conversation he recognised.

'Ice cream!'

And for both of them it was a relief. She could turn away, take time to find her purse again.

'There's a queue at the ice-cream cart,' Luc said, and she could tell by his voice he was as… discombobulated as she was. 'You'll be okay with Toby if it takes a while?'

'Yes.' She shouldn't have snapped but she couldn't help it.

'Of course. I shouldn't have asked.'

'No.' She bit her lip. 'I… Yeah, I have a cast on my leg so if Toby runs I could be in trouble.' She glanced around the beach and saw a cluster of young mums and their toddlers not too far away. 'But if he does I'll yell for help. I've learned to ask for help if I need it, Luc. So thank you for worrying but I'm fine.'

The ice creams were wonderful. They took turns keeping a hand on Toby's wrist to make sure his ice cream didn't get dunked in his water-hole—that'd be a disaster of epic proportions—and licked their own.

There was little need for words. The sun was on their faces and it was all about sensory plea-sure—the warm sand, the hush-hush of the surf, the happy slurps of a toddler in his version of heaven.

People walking along the water's edge turned to smile at them and Luc knew exactly what they were thinking.

A young mum with a broken ankle. Dad tak-ing time to care for her and care for his young son. A family.

It was make-believe, pretend, but for now it felt fine.

Eight years ago… If he'd stayed with Beth… It wouldn't have had to be pretend. He could have been a family man by now. They could have had two or three kids. Living happily ever after.

How could he have kept them all safe?

He suddenly remembered a conversation he and Beth had had, just before she'd walked out.

'I want it all, Luc. I want to go back to medicine. And I want a family. Kids. Maybe even a dog.'

'What the hell…' He still remembered the feeling of panic. 'Beth, I can't even keep you safe.'

'You wouldn't have to keep me safe,' she'd retorted. 'Except in so much as you love me. I'll keep myself safe. There'll be times when I need you—of course there will—isn't that what marriage is all about? But there'll also be times when you need me. And it'll be the same for our kids and this mythical dog I'm proposing. Yes, they'll need us but we'll need them, too. And that's what I'm aching for. Luc, I need to go back to medicine. And I need a family. I've been dependent since my illness and I'm over it. You have to let me care, too.'

He couldn't. The thought of a baby…of Beth being home alone with an infant… For heaven's sake, anything could happen.

'You've told me about your cousin,' she'd said, gently then. 'And I know about your mum. I understand, honestly I do. You know my feelings on it but you can't smother me in caring to make up for it.'

And a month later she'd left.

'You've been wonderful but I no longer need a carer. I need you as my husband but if I can't have one without the other… Luc, I know you can't understand but I need me more than I need you.'

He still didn't fully understand, but as he sat on the sand and watched Toby's unadulterated happiness, he thought maybe he'd been wrong about the family thing. Maybe he could have included children—or at least one child—into his caring. If that could have made Beth happy.

For she was happy now. Toby had misdirected his ice cream and jammed it on his nose. He was snorting rainbow ice cream and giggling, and Beth was chuckling as she tried to sort the situation. She was sitting on the sand, her moon boot protected with a towel so she didn't get sand in her dressings. She was wearing a crimson dress, simple, something the patient welfare people had found her because she couldn't get into the jeans her friends from Namborra had sent. Her hair was still its glorious chestnut. She was wearing prescription sunglasses but they'd slipped down her nose, making her look…adorably cute.

This woman was ten years older than the woman he'd married but she still looked…

'We'd best go home,' she said, breaking the

moment. 'I've found with Toby it's best to quit while we're ahead. One minute you have happiness personified, the next you're in tired territory and, believe me, Luc, you don't want to be there.'

'Hey, I've cared for him for a week.'

'You mean you've seen it.'

'Oh, I've seen it.'

'And yet you've stuck with us. You're a man in a million, Luc Braxton. How many men would take their ex-wives in, no questions asked? No strings?' She smiled happily at him, seemingly totally relaxed. 'You're being wonderful.'

'I'm being useful.'

'Yeah, and you love that.' She put a finger on his nose, a gesture he remembered from all those years ago, a gesture that almost did his head in. 'Okay, friend Luc, let's get this baby to bed. Only… I'm afraid you'll have to carry me again.'

So he did. He carried her over the sand while Toby staggered along gamely, clutching his spade and a handful of sand and the soggy remains of an excellent rainbow ice cream.

Friend Luc.

But that wasn't what he felt like. He didn't feel like a friend at all.

CHAPTER SIX

TWO DAYS LATER he went back to work. At Beth's insistence. She had things under control.

Sort of.

Harriet had introduced her to Alice, a lovely, grandmotherly soul who lived in the same apartment block as Luc. Alice was delighted to offer childcare while Beth did rehab. Beth wheeled her chair there easily, taking the lift, balancing Toby on her knee. Despite being well into her seventies, Alice was almost as bouncy as Toby, so he expended his energy there, and Beth picked him up just as he was about to crash. Then she'd bring him back to Luc's apartment and they'd both nap.

Luc timed his work. He was available for Code One emergencies only, and limited time in ER, so he was home early enough to take them both to the beach before dinner.

'There's no need,' Beth told him, but there was a need. She was so close…

He needed to be with her while he could. He was increasingly aware that she was trying to sort her future in her head and that future didn't include him.

'But I don't think I can go back to Namborra,' she confided, late on the third night. 'I don't think I can work without Ron.'

'Why not?'

'Rules,' she said, flatly, not bitterly. It was simply stating what was. 'My eyesight's not up to standard. Maryanne Clarkson's the other doctor in town and she's a stickler for perfection. When Ron and I approached her to do the combined job she was appalled that we both had health issues. Ron had arthritis that affected his joints—he had to use me to do fine work like finding a tricky vein. Which I could using my magnifying lenses.

'Then Maryanne saw me bump into a post in the car park one night and she rang the medical board the next day and said she doubted my ability to work. I copped a rigid assessment—

which I passed—but she's been looking askance at the pair of us ever since. We've provided an excellent service but I doubt she'll support me without Ron, even though the town was desperate for more doctors before we went and will be desperate again now.'

'It'll be a month before you need to make that decision.'

'Yes,' she said bleakly. 'And for that month Namborra will only have Maryanne and she doesn't do house calls...'

'You and Ron did house calls?'

'Don't say it like it's a criminal act.' She glared.

'Beth, working in a clinic where you know where everything is is one thing but—'

'But there's the elephant again. Beth's blind. *Beth is not blind.*'

But he could see Maryanne's view on this one and it was doing no one a kindness pretending there wasn't an issue. 'You must have trouble,' he said reasonably. 'One of the biggest problems with house calls is that people have lousy lighting.'

'So they do,' she said through gritted teeth.

'And I don't drive so Ron and I did house calls together. And you know what? We had fun. So not only have I lost a friend, I've lost my job and I've lost…fun. Freedom. Dignity. And we did good. No, we did great, so don't you dare imply we were wrong to do it. Leave me be, Luc Braxton. I'm going to bed.'

And he was left, sitting alone watching the moon rise over the sea. Trying to get his head in order.

The phone rang.

Yay for phones, he thought. Yay for work. And it *was* work, a callout to a fire in a holiday rental farmhouse twenty minutes away by chopper.

'An explosion.' Mabel was curt. 'It'll be a meths lab or something like that. It always is. Explosion in remote rented farmhouse. Kids everywhere. What were they thinking?'

'Idea of casualties?' He had his phone tucked under his chin, pulling his boots on as he talked. He wasn't in the business of making judgements. He was in the business of cleaning up afterwards.

'Multiple. Two probable deaths, but no proper

count at this stage. It's miles from anywhere. A neighbour rang it in, sounding sensible but overwhelmed. Says most of the kids seem drug affected, even if they're not injured. The local cop's on his way, as are the local paramedics and fire brigade but they'll need backup.'

'I'll be on the chopper in three minutes,' Luc said, and disconnected. And turned to find Beth watching him from the bedroom door. Leaning on her crutches.

'Trouble?'

'Kids, drugs and fire,' he said abruptly, grabbing his bag. 'An appalling combination and all too common. You'll be all right here while I'm gone?'

'I'll try and hold it together.' Even in his rush he could hear the edge of bitterness in her voice. 'If I didn't have Toby I'd be with you.'

'Yeah, with a broken leg and—'

'Let's not go there,' she snapped. 'Stay safe, Luc.' And before he knew what she intended she hopped across to where he stood and kissed him lightly on the cheek. 'Go save everyone I can't. Do it for me.'

He shouldn't respond. There was no time for anything except getting to the roof to board the chopper.

Except some things were imperative.

Somehow he found himself holding her, gripping her shoulders, looking down into her troubled eyes.

Soldier going into battle? Farewelling his woman? That was fanciful. This was not his woman. Beth was part of his past, nothing more. But still…

Still the need was imperative.

He'd heard the anger in her voice. He couldn't leave her like this, and he reacted the only way he knew how.

He bent his head and kissed her, hard and strong, taking what he needed from the feel of her body against him, the fleeting melting of her breasts against his chest, the instant rush of response. Telling her he was sorry. Telling her his concern was because…because he didn't understand anything any more.

And then he pulled away because he must, and she pulled away, too.

No choice.

'Stay safe,' she said again, but this time it was a shaken whisper.

'For you,' he said, just as shakily, and then he was gone and Beth was left staring at a closed door.

Wondering what had just happened to make her feel her life had changed all over again.

Blake was off duty. Luc was in charge and he flew into a disaster.

What on earth made kids think they could set up a chemical lab a highly qualified scientist would worry about, following dodgy instructions on even more dodgy internet websites, trying to make drugs when they had no knowledge of the composite ingredients—and doing it when they were half-stoned?

The farmhouse was obviously being used as party central. The chopper landed and they could see a dying bonfire in the paddock beside the house, bottles and cans everywhere as if a party had been in full swing for a few days—and a weatherboard farmhouse that had burned so fast that the ruins were starting to smoulder rather than burn.

It looked like it was—a disaster, Luc thought grimly, as they took in the scene from the air.

There was one police car, lights flashing, parked at the gate beside an ambulance—the type used by volunteer, rural paramedics. The local fire engine was on the scene but no one seemed to be trying to put a fire out. The two firemen seemed occupied with injured kids.

The chopper Luc was in was a big one, holding the lead firies as well as the medic crew. Kev looked down grimly. 'This'll be forensic stuff,' he muttered. 'Hell, it must have burned hot. We'll be lucky if we get anything for mums and dads to bury.'

Luc cast him a sympathetic glance. Kev had seen everything in a career that spanned over forty years but he still wasn't inured to the sort of catastrophe below.

Nobody in the team was.

They didn't speak as they came in to land. They were shocked at what they were seeing but their silence wasn't caused by shock.

This team was a well-oiled machine, honed by years of response to catastrophes like this and worse. Every man and woman would be doing a personal assessment of what lay underneath them, checking the groups of kids clustered around obvious casualties, seeing how some kids were still close to the fire. For heaven's sake, why hadn't the firies got them back? Even though the fire had burned down, if it was a suspect meth lab there may well be more stuff in there liable to explode. There must be severely injured kids to hold their attention.

'Sam, you're on triage,' Luc snapped as the chopper finally came to rest and the team unclipped and grabbed their gear. 'Gina?' he called to the chopper pilot. 'Radio in with request for backup, a couple of med. evacuation choppers with every paramedic they can find. I'm seeing ten kids on the ground from here. People, we're dealing with drugs as well as injuries so watch yourself. Even the kids who are uninjured are likely to be volatile. Try and work in pairs, covering your backs. Right, go.'

How could she sleep?

She lay in bed and turned on the radio. The late-night jocks were all over it. Explosion in a remote farmhouse. Casualty count rising. Four dead. How many did that mean injured?

She was lying in bed, warm, safe with her little boy beside her. Her leg was aching. She had the drugs to fix it but she didn't feel like fixing it.

She wanted to be out and doing. In the middle of the action. Working beside Luc, making a difference as she'd longed to all her life.

What chance now? Namborra would be closed to her. She'd have months off work with her leg and then the fight would start all over again to get herself accepted.

While others put themselves in harm's way, doing the work she longed for?

The latest news flash—updating the death count to five.

She felt ill.

At dawn Toby stirred. At least that gave her something to do. She got him breakfast, played with him for a while and then headed to rehab.

Harriet was there, stoically lifting her foot, grim-faced, trying desperately to get her leg working.

It would never be completely normal, Beth

thought. Luc had told her just how much damage Harriet had suffered.

Harriet was looking at a lifetime disability, too.

Beth settled herself on the mat beside Harriet and waited while the physiotherapist braced her leg.

Both women concentrated fiercely on their exercises for a while, saying nothing. Then…

'I hate it,' Harriet said, and she sounded close to tears.

'Because you should be out there, too?'

'Of course I should,' Harriet said bitterly. 'But they're saying I'll have to accept a degree of weakness. They'll never let me back on the team. At least your ankle will get better.'

'You think Luc would ever let me near his precious team with my eyesight?'

'Yeah, and he still thinks of you as family. It's a wonder he hadn't put you in a cotton wool climate controller and put the setting to safe.'

'You do understand him,' Beth said cautiously.

'The whole team knows Luc. If there's danger, there's Luc. It almost kills him if someone else has to take a risk. He'd care for the whole world.'

'I hope to hell there's no risk where he is now.'

'Even if there is, you wouldn't be allowed to share.' Harriet gave her leg a savage jerk upward, which earned her a sharp rebuke from the physiotherapist.

'Easy, Harriet. And you, too, Beth. Don't try and walk before you can run. You need to accept your limitations.'

'Of course we do,' Harriet retorted, and Beth grimaced.

'Of course,' Beth muttered. 'And if we forget, all we need to do is ask Luc.'

By early evening Toby was more than ready for sleep. He seemed a bit listless, out of sorts, and so was Beth. No matter how much she hated it, her body needed rest to recover. She'd hardly slept last night, she'd done a decent rehab session and by the time Toby fell asleep Beth was ready to do the same.

There was still no sign of Luc. She'd heard the first casualties had been flown in but there was still work to be done on the ground.

She had soup on the stove in case he appeared.

There was nothing more she could do, for him, for anyone.

She headed for the bedroom she shared with Toby, put her head on the pillow and slept.

And woke as a cat did, at the first sound, as the door opened inward just a little.

'Luc?'

'It's okay.' It was barely a whisper. He clearly had no intention of waking Toby—or waking her? 'Go back to sleep.'

As if she could. She tossed back the covers, grabbed her glasses and crutches and hobbled out.

He was leaning heavily against the kitchen counter. He looked…appalling.

He'd stripped off his protective gear before coming home but there must have been red dust and smoke where he was because it had infiltrated everything. He was wearing jeans and a T-shirt and the coarse sand was caked on. The lines on his chest where his T-shirt had tugged over his pecs, where he'd sweated, formed a road map of red dirt.

And the rest… His thick, black hair was matted with dust and soot. He'd have worn gloves but the dust had got through, staining his hands. He stank of smoke and other things that were indescribable. The lines on his face…the matted stubble on his jaw… That was shocking enough but what was worse was his eyes. They were… haggard, mired in fatigue and distress.

'Bad?' she whispered, even though it was a dumb question. His eyes told of a nightmare.

'Kids.' He closed his eyes as if he couldn't bear to go there. 'Schoolies. Kids who've finished their last exam. They hired the house, told their parents they were going camping…yeah, I know they were mostly eighteen but what parent sends them off without checking? So drugs and alcohol, and more drugs and alcohol and who knew what else besides? And then two imbeciles who thought they were ants' pants in the chemistry world decided they'd make their own gear. They'd bought the stuff on the internet and brought it with them, waiting until everyone was half-stoned to show off their new skill. Half the kids seem to have been in the kitchen when it exploded. Five dead and that's not the worst. There are kids who'll carry the physical scars for life and every one of them will carry the mental scars.'

'Oh, Luc...'

He put his hands up and raked his fingers through his matted hair, then buried his head in his hands. 'What were their parents thinking?' His voice was muffled with pain. 'What the hell...?'

And she couldn't bear it. She dropped her crutches. She had no remembrance later of how she supported herself to reach him. All she knew was that she did. She folded her arms around him and tugged him into her, tight, hard, and she held him and held him and held him.

At first he didn't yield, seemingly locked in his own personal horror. For a moment she thought he'd pull away. Maybe he'd slam out the door as he'd done sometimes in the past when he'd been distressed and he couldn't bear to let her see.

He protected others from pain; he didn't share it.

But holding was all she could do. Of course it wasn't enough. He didn't need her. This man didn't need anyone and surely she should know it.

But still she held, hard, tight, willing his pain

to crack. To open the armour just a little and take comfort...

And then he shuddered, an involuntary spasm that shook his whole body, that shook hers, and he buried his face in her hair and groaned. Or sobbed? It was a guttural sound of total anguish and she thought, Oh, Luc, what have you seen? How are such things bearable? How can you keep caring and caring, rescuing and rescuing and holding the horrors to yourself?

But the sob seemed to have released something deep within. His hands came around her waist and tugged her against him, harder than she was holding him. Pulling her into him. Seeking the warmth and strength of her body.

'Beth...' It was a groan from the depths of need. 'Beth...'

'Hush, love,' she whispered. and reached up and ran her fingers through his hair, through the dust, sweat and grime. She didn't mind— how could she mind? Her hands drew his head down, so she could kiss the dust from his eyes. Her fingers held, possessive. This man was in such pain.

Her man.

And that's how it felt. Ten years ago she'd made vows that should have been dissolved by a divorce court but they were suddenly all around her now.

To love and to honour… In sickness and in health…

I, Beth, take thee, Luc…

And she was taking him now, holding him, willing him to yield to her with every ounce of hope and prayer left in her. Her Luc, her own Luc…

'Beth…' And when he said her name this time it was different. It was like a voice coming from the darkest of places but seeing a glimmer of light. Just a glimmer but that was all she asked.

'Luc,' she whispered, and tugged his head closer, down, so she could touch his lips. Take him to her. Heal with her body.

And take what was hers?

For there was a part of her that knew it was her right to comfort this man, that taking his pain into her was the way it should be.

Had her wedding vows been indeed unbreakable? That was how it felt right now, as if the vows held true. That he was part of her and he was suffering, hurting, holding so much pain inside that she couldn't bear it, and if it was in her to comfort then that's what she must do.

Because his pain felt like hers.

She felt him stiffen again, just slightly as she tugged him down, as her mouth found his, and for a fraction of a second she was terrified he'd pull away. No, she wanted to shout. You have no right to pull away. You have no right to keep your pain to yourself for it's mine, too. She didn't say it—she couldn't because her mouth was claiming his, searching, demanding and every minuscule part of her was a prayer.

Let me in. Luc, let me share...

And she felt it, the moment when the tension eased, as if the pressure had built up to the point where containment was impossible. He groaned again but it was different. This was suddenly not a man fighting himself.

He wanted her. She knew that, she'd always known that, but this was more. For the first time ever, he was drawing into her for comfort.

For need?

But now there was no time for introspection. No time for wonder. Because she was being held, kissed, taken with an urgency, a passion that left room for nothing else.

He was lifting her, and the dreadful blankness in his eyes was changing. His eyes were darkening, with desire, with passion, with need. He held her high, pulling her against his chest. She was wearing…okay, nothing very sexy, in fact the opposite. She'd taken off her dress when she'd fallen into bed and she was now wearing her glasses, a moon boot, a nice, sensible bra and panties, bought from the discount store at Namborra, and an ancient wrap. Not a sexy inch of lace anywhere. But the look Luc was giving her…

So much for sexy negligees. Total waste, she thought with a stab of satisfaction and for some dumb reason she found herself chuckling.

'What?' He'd started striding toward his bedroom, his arms full of her, but he stopped at the sound of her chuckle. His dark eyes gleamed down at her, and her heart twisted with love and with desire.

After all these years… Her Luc…

'The chuckle…' he managed. 'What's funny?'

'I was just thinking of pure silk negligees and…'

'Don't.' He groaned again. 'Beth, you're driving me wild.' And then he stopped as if sense had suddenly reared its head and he had to force himself to say it. 'Love...are you sure?'

'I guess...' Somehow she had to force herself to say it, too. 'If you can... If you have...'

And he got that, too. He'd always had the unnerving ability to read her mind.

'What doctor doesn't carry condoms for educational purposes? But you'll have to wait until I'm showered. If I hit the sheets like this we'll have to buy new linen.'

'Worth it, love.'

'Then worth waiting,' he said, and grinned. 'If you didn't have a leg covered in dressings and a moon boot...'

'And if you didn't have half the outback splattered on your person...'

'All I need is three minutes.' He lowered her onto the bed.

'You can have two,' she told him. 'I've waited for eight years and I won't wait a moment longer.'

She didn't need to.

CHAPTER SEVEN

THEY HAD A night of blessed peace. A night when the work receded.

And then the world flooded back, and then some.

They'd slept after making love, skin against skin, lost in the wonder of each other's bodies.

They were woken by a sound of distress that had Beth tossing back the covers and reaching for her glasses and wrap before she even remembered where she was.

Luc woke, too. They'd been spooned together as they'd slept all those years ago, encased in each other's bodies. At home. At peace. Now he moved with her, his hand still on her thigh. 'Love? What?'

'Toby.'

'I guess that's the new norm,' he said sleepily, as she reached for her wrap. 'Being woken by a baby.' But then he jerked wide awake.

He got it. He'd been looking after Toby for a week while she'd been in hospital. He knew Toby's normal was to wake up happy. As long as Robert Rabbit was in the cot with him he'd burble and chat and play until his mother got her act together and got them both out of there.

If Robert had fallen out, then Toby roared, a full-throated yell of indignation, but what they were hearing now was a reedy whimper, and it had Beth grabbing her crutches and heading for the door fast.

Luc was right behind her, hauling on his pants as he came.

Toby was lying in the cot, uttering little mews of distress. He was on his back, staring at the ceiling. Robert Rabbit lay unheeded by his side.

As Beth reached the cot he registered her presence and held his arms up, as if pleading. Get me out of here?

Why wasn't he standing?

Beth's crutches clattered to the floor as she scooped him up and Luc shoved a chair forward so she could sit with him.

She cradled him against her, a tousle-headed toddler, usually a bright, happy baby version of Beth herself. But now he crumpled into her, limp, miserable. The weak sobs stopped.

Years ago, back when Luc had been an intern, green about the gills, he remembered a child being brought into the emergency department roaring so loudly every head had swivelled to see what was wrong. Luc had responded automatically, turning from the child he'd been treating.

He'd been brought up short by his consultant, an elderly doctor who'd been practising paediatrics since before Luc had been born.

'Stay where you are,' she'd snapped. 'There's no emergency. If a child can roar like that then any damage is superficial. For kids' triage, you see to the silent ones first.'

But now… Toby was silent.

'He's hot,' Beth said, kissing his forehead. 'A virus?'

That'd explain it. Kids got ill fast and they got better fast, too. Nothing to worry about.

Except the silence. And the limpness.

He knelt and put his fingers on Toby's neck. Yeah, definitely hot. They needed to get him cool.

And the way he held himself…he was huddled

on his mother's knees but his head wasn't tucked down. He was pulling to one side.

As if his neck hurt?

Luc unzipped his sleeping bag—and froze.

'What?' Beth whispered and Luc rose and pulled back the curtains, flooding the room with dawn light. So Beth could see what he was seeing.

She saw. 'Oh, God…' It was scarcely spoken, a breath of sheer terror. 'Oh…'

'Hey, he's in the right place.' Luc was already heading for his phone. 'I'll ring in and warn them we're coming. It might not be…'

'It is.' She didn't move, stunned with the horror of what she faced. 'Luc…the day of the crash… When I went to pick him up from crèche they asked me to see another child. A rash… A high temp. I started him on antibiotics and got him on a plane to Sydney before the diagnosis was confirmed but I was pretty sure it was meningitis. I left instructions…the minute we had confirmation I wanted the kids he'd been in contact with started on prophylactic antibiotics. And then… Oh, God, Luc, I forgot. I forgot…'

She broke on a sob.

He was on the phone, kneeling beside her, doing his darnedest to be there for Beth, for both of them, even as he barked into the receiver. Marsha was head of Paediatrics and she was the best. At least they were in the right spot. If this was what they thought it was then Toby was in the best place in Australia. 'We have a twenty-month-old with suspected meningitis. We're bringing him in now. Ten minutes.'

'Your little boy?'

Marsha's demand gave him pause even then. The hospital grapevine had indeed done its job. He'd gone to Namborra and brought back a woman who was his ex-wife. He'd taken time off and cared for her child and now he was living with her.

Your little boy?

He looked at Toby, at this little stranger he hadn't met until ten days ago.

He looked at Toby's mother.

'Yes,' he said.

As a doctor he'd always had some inkling that waiting was hard. He'd seen relatives in hundreds of settings during his career, white faced, limp with fear. Often it had been Luc who'd opened the door on that waiting room to give news, sometimes good, sometimes bleak, sometimes terrible.

Now it was his turn.

He shouldn't be here. He was officially on duty. He hoped someone had noticed where he was and told Blake. He'd made one urgent call as they'd arrived, one that couldn't wait, but that was all he'd had time for. All his focus was on Toby.

The way the rash had spread over Toby's small body... The spike in his temperature...the look on the paediatricians' faces as they'd assessed... It had stilled him to numbness.

Was it better to not know the odds? Was it better to not know the risk of appalling long-term damage?

He sat with Beth while they inserted IV lines, set up the antibiotics, maximum dosages. They had fluid lines going in, because by now Toby was too weak to drink. Indeed he seemed barely conscious. The illness was taking over so fast...

Beth sat and held as much as she could of him and Luc stayed in the background. And waited.

He watched the tension of Beth's shoulders, he watched her mouth move in silent prayer, he watched her fingers curl around Toby's as if by sheer force of will she could hold him. As if she could keep him safe. He watched as they insisted on transferring him to a bed so they could work more intensely. He watched Beth watch her baby. He watched for hours.

Finally Marsha ordered him to take Beth out. 'Take half an hour,' she said, and stooped to take Beth's hands firmly in hers. Toby lay on a too big bed, IV lines taped, his tiny face blotched and pallid as he lay among a sea of high-tech monitors. 'Beth, Toby's asleep. For now he doesn't need you.'

'He's un—' Beth began.

'He's not unconscious. This looks a natural sleep.'

'But—'

'But he needs you when he wakes,' Marsha told her. 'And you're no use to him if you fall over. I'm working in here for the next half-hour and the nurses will be here, too. We'll watch him like a hawk and the moment there's any change, the moment he opens his eyes, I'll call you back.

Luc, take Beth into the waiting room. There's coffee and sandwiches. Bully her to eat. Bully her to take time out. Do anything, but take a break from the tension. Now.'

So here they were, in the tiny waiting room outside kids' intensive care unit. The room contained a drinks vending machine. An overhead television, turned on but no sound. No windows.

Take a break from the tension? It was impossible. He knew Beth couldn't leave the hospital and he had the sense not to suggest it.

'I can't bear it,' Beth whispered. She'd managed a sandwich and coffee but he knew it had been sheer strength of will that'd got the food down. 'I need to go back.'

'Marsha will have my hide if I let you back in before half an hour,' Luc told her. 'She's good, Beth. The whole team's good. I suspect she'll have half the hospital's paediatric team in there pooling their knowledge while she has a parent-free zone.'

'I wouldn't interfere...'

'But you know as well as I do that a parent's distress can sometimes mess with doctors' heads. Especially with children. We need to give them space, Beth. For the best outcome.'

She picked up another sandwich, stared at it and then set it down again. 'I can't believe… He was so well…'

And then she stood, so fast her empty mug of coffee clattered to the floor and smashed. She didn't notice. Her eyes were huge and her face had lost its last trace of colour. 'The other kids,' she whispered, her voice loaded with horror. 'In crèche. I set up orders to follow up. As soon as Felix's diagnosis was confirmed they were to start… And then I forgot. It won't be just Toby. Luc, the others…'

He tried to hug her, pulling her against him, but she held rigid. 'I can't… Luc, if I hurt them…'

'You haven't hurt anyone,' he said, solidly now, putting her back until he could look into her haunted eyes. 'They're fine. The crèche was un-damaged so no other child was hurt. You might not have noticed but as soon as Toby was ad-mitted, I left you for a moment. While Marsha was doing initial assessment and setting up the first IV lines, I rang Namborra. I spoke to Dr Clarkson. She said Margie remembered—the head of your crèche? She had the presence of mind to take the crèche notes with her when the centre was evacuated. Your orders were the last ones written and she realised they were impor-tant. By next morning every kid who'd been in crèche was started on prophylactic antibiotics. Dr Clarkson's gutted they didn't follow up on Toby.'

'So Toby's the only one I forgot...'

She was close to collapse. He dragged her back into his arms, holding her, feeling her body shudder with tension and fear. 'Beth, listen. You didn't forget Toby. You sheltered him with your body as the roof collapsed. You saved Toby.'

'What use is that if he dies from meningitis? Or loses his legs or arms? You know what men-ingitis can do. I can't—'

'Beth!' He put her back again, holding her firmly by her shoulders, forcing her gaze to meet his. 'Firstly, Toby's already been immun-ised so you did your best by protecting him all you could. We don't know what strain this is but maybe the protection he already has will help now. Dr Clarkson tells me Felix, who you diag-nosed on the day you were trapped, has made a full recovery. She's organised parental consent so details of the strain he had have been faxed here. Our medical team's already working with full information.'

'Second, he's been caught fast. I checked on Toby an hour after...after we went to bed.' He touched her cheek, smiling faintly at the memory. 'Things were too new, too overwhelming for me to sleep, and for some reason...' He hesitated. 'For some reason I needed to ground myself and seeing Toby helped. He was sleeping peacefully, clutching Wobit. Therefore, whatever this is, it's come on fast but we've caught it fast, too. We've also caught it within ten minutes of one of the best paediatric units in Australia. The doctors here are the best. He'll be fine, Beth, I know it.'

He couldn't know it, not for sure, but he put every ounce of conviction into his voice, into his body language. His eyes didn't leave hers. She gazed up at him and he saw the moment a faint chink broke through the flood of terror.

'You really think so?'

'I know.'

She didn't break her gaze. 'You checked on him while I slept?'

'As I said, I sort of…needed to. And I've been doing it for the week you've been in hospital.'

'You checked on him through the night when you were caring for him?'

'Before you came home I had his cot in my room.'

'Oh, Luc…' She sobbed and gasped and then buried her face into his shirt, hard, fierce, as if she needed the sheer bulk of him to assure herself all was well. Or all would be well.

'I told myself I didn't need you,' she whispered, half to herself, half to him. 'All those years ago. I thought I didn't need you and how wrong was that? How stupid? Oh, love…'

And she put her hands around him as if she'd never let go.

He hugged her back, solidly, tugging her against him so her breasts moulded against his chest, kissing her hair, saying dumb, meaningless nothings because she didn't need silence.

She needed…him.

And part of him wanted it. Part of him held her and thought his world was settling. He had his woman back in his bed, in his life. She was his wife. And Toby? The little boy already felt like his own.

'Beth?'

'Mmm...' It was a whisper, no more.

'Tell me about...' It almost broke him to say it, but it needed to be asked. 'Toby's father.'

'Wh-why? Her face was muffled in his shirt.

'He needs to be told.' That was the truth, he thought. If it was *his* son he'd want to be told he was in danger.

He wanted it to be his son.

'You mean...he might die...'

'Beth...'

'I know.' She pushed away, shoving her curls from her tear-streaked face. 'I know...the odds. But I don't need to tell him.'

'Why not, Beth?'

'Toby's...from donated sperm. After you...' She shook her head. 'Crazy but after you I couldn't imagine being married to anyone else. But I thought...when I started work at Namborra, I thought I could care for a baby. I thought...' Her voice broke. 'Oh, God, Luc, I was so wrong.'

'You weren't wrong.' He said it strongly. He

might not believe it himself but she didn't need a talk on responsibility now. 'You had a fantastic set-up. You had everything in place to care for him.'

'But I couldn't care for him. When I walked away from you I felt so brave, like I could take on the world. But to put Toby at risk...'

'It wasn't your fault.'

'You never would have let it happen.' Her voice broke on another ragged sob and she buried her face in his shirt again. 'Oh, Luc, we needed you. I needed you...'

And wasn't that what he needed to hear?

He held her close as her sobs subsided, as she fought to regain composure, as she fought to regain control of her world. But still she clung.

She needed him.

She'd held him. She'd lain in his arms. She was his wife again, in every sense of the word, and part of him felt like a vast void inside him had been filled. His Beth was where she belonged, and Toby with her.

He would care for them, he vowed. He'd love them and protect them for ever, he told himself as he held her close.

But there was another voice, a tiny insidious crazy voice that told him something was wrong.

Nothing's wrong, he told himself or nothing will be wrong as long as Toby survives unscathed. This was how things should be. This was his family and he could love and protect them for ever.

So why was the little voice niggling?

Why did he feel…something was still very wrong and it had nothing to do with Toby's illness?

For two days Beth and Luc watched and waited, two adults with only one thought between them. That Toby survive with no long-term damage.

For two days he lay limp, almost unresponsive. For two days the doctors fought with everything they had.

And won.

On the afternoon of the third day Luc closed his eyes for a few moments and the miracle happened. He woke to find Beth cuddling Toby. The little boy still had his IV lines attached, but his eyes were wide, he looked alert and he was struggling to pull himself away from Beth's arms.

'Walk,' he said firmly, and Beth closed her eyes for a nanosecond and let him slide to the floor.

The drip lines were still attached but Beth had them organised so he couldn't pull them free.

Toby tried to stand but his legs didn't hold him. The days of desperate illness would have made the strongest individual's knees turn to jelly. So he plonked on the floor in his nappy and singlet, staring at his legs as if he couldn't believe they'd let him down. And then he glanced around the room and saw Luc. He gave a joyful chirp and hauled himself into a crawl position.

Crawling worked. He made a bee-line to his playmate of a week. He and Luc had dug a hole almost to China and his body language said hooray, take him there again. He reached Luc's ankles and held up his hands.

Luc rose and gathered him into his arms, while Beth wrangled IV lines. And Luc buried his face into Toby's small, bony shoulder and felt...like bursting into tears.

It was okay.

But Toby wasn't in the mood for hugs. He'd had a very long sleep, he was in a hospital room full of interesting *things* and he wanted down. So Luc set him back down. Toby found an oxygen canister he'd really like to unscrew—how did these things work?—and Luc had time and space to hug Toby's mother.

'Over,' he said softly into her hair, and he touched her face and felt tears slipping down. So many tears over the last few days… His strong Beth… Even when she'd been desperately ill herself he could never remember tears, but now… Toby's illness seemed to have undercut every foundation she had.

'I can't say… I can't imagine…if you hadn't been here…if you hadn't taken us in…'

'Not so much of the gratitude,' he growled. 'I think…we're family, Beth. And family cares.'

'After all this time…' She drew back and stared at him wonderingly. 'Is that how you feel?'

'I've never stopped loving you.' He knew that for truth—he'd known it the moment he'd seen her under the rubble. *Until death us do part.* He'd made that vow and it seemed burned into his psyche. Maybe it always had been. Since Beth, he'd never had a serious long-term partner.

Because he already was married?

'I think… Luc, I still love you, too,' she managed.

And he thought, Dammit, she's even weaker than her son. She'd hardly eaten for the last three days. She'd almost worn herself out with fear, and she sure as hell hadn't slept. He hugged her against him and felt her sink into him.

It was where she should be. Where he could care.

And the words were out before he could stop himself. 'Beth, maybe we should think about getting ourselves married again.'

He'd tried—desperately—to keep his voice light but she stepped back and looked up at him. The suggestion hadn't been made lightly at all and she knew it. The bonds between them were still strong and he saw that she knew it as truly as he did.

'Luc…it must be too soon.' She turned away, giving herself space, looking almost panicked. She gazed down at Toby, who was starting to get seriously annoyed that the oxygen cylinder wouldn't open to his command. 'And Toby…'

'I love Toby already. It would be my honour to love and protect you both.'

'And you need someone to love and protect...' She closed her eyes. 'Oh, Luc, if I could be sure you weren't sacrificing...'

'How can I be sacrificing, marrying for love?'

She shook her head as if clearing fog. 'We need you.' She sounded as if she was talking to herself. 'I thought I was so self-sufficient, yet at the first hurdle...'

'It's hardly the first hurdle,' he told her. 'You've completed your medical degree. You found a job you were good at, and you and Ron have been providing Namborra a great little medical service.'

'Little...' She faltered. 'Sorry, I know... I need to accept...' She took a deep breath and went to lift Toby. She was still wearing her protective boot and she staggered, off balance. He was there in a nanosecond, hugging her against him, supporting her, with Toby somewhere in the middle.

'We don't have to decide yet,' he told her. 'Think about it.'

Think.

She should pull away, she thought, but he was supporting her.

She had a broken ankle.

She had a broken will.

It would be so easy to sink into Luc's arms, to let him take charge as he'd taken charge when she'd lost her sight, to admit that she wanted him and…she needed him.

Luc had been right all those years ago when he'd said she should accept her limitations. And it wasn't one way, she thought. Luc needed her to need him. It gave him strength and security to know that he was helping. She knew all about his painful childhood. She knew all about how helpless he felt when those he loved weren't safe.

So why was she hesitating? Why didn't she fall into his arms with a yes when she knew he needed her as much as she needed him?

But she wasn't hesitating, she told herself. She was simply giving him time to figure what he really wanted. To be free or have a permanent millstone around his neck.

A woman who'd tried and failed.

'Hey.' He'd always known what she was thinking and now seemed no exception. He guided her back into the chair and knelt before her. 'Beth, this isn't the end of the world. You're seeing things at their bleakest now, even though Toby's getting better. But your leg still hurts. I bet it's hurting now. You've hardly eaten and you haven't slept for three days. Give yourself a break. Let's do what we need for Toby and then let's get you some rest. In the next few days you can look at this again and decide whether what I'm suggesting is sensible. It's sure as hell not a failure.'

'No,' she managed, and hugged Toby and went to say something else.

Except the door was opening and Marsha entered, followed by a couple of med students.

'I'm here to boast about my success story to my students,' she said, beaming down at Toby. 'I guess you guys are pretty happy, huh?'

'We surely are,' Beth said, and hugged Toby still tighter. 'All is...perfect.'

Luc wanted to marry her again. The concept was mind-blowing.

She could have another baby, she thought suddenly. It would be Luc's this time, not a sperm donor. If Luc thought she'd be able to cope... If he thought it was okay...

'Everything's looking good,' Luc told Marsha but his gaze was still on Beth. 'Our little family's looking safe.'

'Your family?' Marsha's eyebrows did an expressive hike. 'Really?'

'If Beth will have me,' he told her, and Beth shook her head.

'I don't think... I doubt if Luc needs...'

'Hey,' Luc said, and lifted Toby from her so Marsha could check his progress for herself. 'Luc doesn't need, but Beth and Toby do. But let's talk about this tomorrow. For now, Toby's fine and we have all the time in the world.'

CHAPTER EIGHT

WHAT FOLLOWED WAS a week almost out of time. Marriage wasn't mentioned again. It was almost as if they were afraid of it. But every night they lay in each other's arms and knew how right it felt.

They still seemed like a tight-knit family. Toby was recovering, but Beth wanted him close. She was subdued but Toby was anything but. The little boy was a blessing, a happy bubble in the face of Beth's confusion.

Luc was trying his best but she wouldn't have him take more time off. 'We'll be right on our own, Luc. It's enough that you're sharing your apartment, that you're helping at night.'

And she did need him. When he got home from work she seemed almost relieved when he took over childcare for a couple of hours. He took Toby to the beach but she didn't come. 'I'm tired,' she told him, and he knew she was.

And at night…she slept in his arms, but that sleep was broken. He wasn't supposed to know that she slipped out of bed and went out to the balcony to stare sightlessly out to sea.

Once he'd gone out to join her and she'd come in straight away. 'I'm sorry. I didn't mean to disturb you.'

And now… He'd come home from a routine shift and found her staring at her email.

'Luc, the memorial service is happening next Monday at Namborra,' she told him. 'And I'd really like to go. For Ron especially. I was in hospital when he was buried so I couldn't be there. But now… I need to be there for this.'

Of course she did and things cleared in Luc's head. Yes, she was depressed, but the fault didn't lie at his door. She'd been injured. Toby had been desperately ill. But on top of that she'd lost her best friend, her colleague. Of course she was down.

'I don't think I can manage…by myself,' she said, and he thought it almost killed her to say it. The flatness…

And he knew the depression wasn't all about

shock and injury and loss of her friend. What else had she lost?

'Of course I'll take you…come with you.' He changed his words but he still saw her flinch. 'We can fly. There's an outback health service operating from Bondi Bayside. The team heads west three days a week. They could drop us off on the way and collect us on the way back.' He tried a smile. 'It's cheaper than commercial flights and if you like you can have a whole bed to lie down on. It'll be better for your leg than sitting up.'

'And if they need to transfer patients?'

'Then we hang around in Namborra until Wednesday. Or take a commercial flight.'

'I still have my apartment at Namborra.'

'Then that's settled. But chances are good we won't need it. Except for a place for you to rest, he thought. She was so tired. She seemed…as if the life had been sucked out of her.

'Thank you, Luc,' she managed, and he hugged her.

'Hey, my pleasure.'

'I know it is. I wish…'

And then she shook her head and managed a

smile. 'No. It's no use wishing. It is what it is. You want to take Toby to the beach?'

'I do,' he told her, and let her go with reluctance to pick up the bubbly Toby. 'Would you like to come with us?'

'I might have a sleep if that's okay with you.'

'Of course it's okay. Beth... I love you.'

'I love you, too,' she whispered, but her face was bleak. And he knew that when he left, she wouldn't sleep at all.

The memorial service for the victims of the plaza disaster was held in Namborra's civic centre. It was a magnificent hall, built with community pride, on the only hill Namborra boasted. It could almost be taken for a modern church, Luc thought, with its soaring ceilings and magnificent stained glass. The glass, though, depicted the heart of Namborra, fields of wheat, sheep grazing in lush pastures, the wild birds that frequented the wetlands behind the town. And behind the stained glass were the very things the windows depicted. Luc looked around him and saw all of Namborra within the hall, and all of Namborra stretching away outside.

The flight had been delayed because of a medical crisis. They'd arrived just as the service was about to begin, but the locals had known Beth was coming and had reserved them space near the front. Margie from the crèche had met them off the chopper. She and Beth had hugged for a long time. When Beth had hobbled into the hall, with Luc carrying Toby behind her, there'd been a massive stir. Those in aisle seats had risen and hugged her, and by the time they reached their seats, Beth's eyes were already moist.

Now they sat side by side. Luc cuddled a blessedly sleepy Toby and held Beth's hand with his free hand as they listened to local after local recounting the stories of lives lost.

First they talked of Bill Mickle, family man, retired plumber, passionate about his beloved greyhounds who never did any good on the track but Bill was always hopeful. Born and bred in Namborra. Five grown kids and three grandies.

An elderly lady stood at the end of Bill's son's spiel and told how Bill had chopped her wood every Thursday night. She sat and wept and Beth sniffed and Luc held her hand tighter.

Toby had been playing with a miniature toy

truck but he'd gone to sleep in Luc's arms. Beth and Luc seemed…a cocoon in the midst of the community's grief.

Except Beth was grief-stricken, too.

Next in line were stories of Ray and Daphne Oddie. Farmers. They'd produced the best scones in the district, and the best merino sheep.

'Ray used to bring me scones whenever he came for his diabetes check,' Beth whispered, sniffing. 'Daphne was always too busy with the sheep to cook. For Ray it meant cook or starve. They worked it out.' She sniffed again and smiled. 'Scones were his forte but you should have tasted his lemon meringue pie. I'd have married him for that.'

She smiled mistily as those on stage went on to talk of a woman called Mariette Goldsworthy, a friend of Ray and Daphne from out of town, but she'd visited enough to be known and liked. She'd been notorious for cleaning up at the local bingo session.

And then… Ron McKenzie. Beth's partner.

His daughter, Faye, rose to speak. Of Ron's early life, his love of living. Of his grief at the loss of his wife. How Namborra had given him his life back and how the family would be grateful for ever.

And how much Ron had loved Beth. 'We were his kids,' Faye told the audience. 'But after Mum died we could do nothing. He was lost in grief but Beth... Beth, you were here when you were needed. What you achieved was a miracle. You gave us our dad back and we'll be grateful for ever. Beth, on Dad's behalf, we thank you. Our last loving memories of our dad will shine because of the joy you gave him.'

There was a moment's silence and then the hall burst into spontaneous applause. It wasn't just for Ron, Luc thought. It was for the woman sitting silently weeping beside him.

The knowledge was suddenly overwhelming. Beth had done this. Not only had she provided a medical service to this town, she'd spread her love. She'd made a community love her.

A kernel of something he hadn't felt before was budding deep inside. Pride? Admiration? Awe?

And then she was standing, tugging on his hand until he released her. Heading to join Faye on stage.

He was still holding the sleeping Toby but others rose to help as she hobbled to the stage.

He sat, stunned. After all she'd gone through, to stand and speak in this packed hall...

But she handed her crutches to the people who'd helped her onto the stage and rested her hands on the lectern, supporting herself so every speck of her concentration was on the people she was talking to.

The people of Namborra.

She spoke of meeting Ron for the first time, of his devotion to his wife, of the privilege of sharing his desolation when she died. She spoke of seeing him at his lowest, surrounded by his family and yet unable to see them. Unable to let them help him. Unable to see anything but his loss.

And then she spoke of Ron's face when he'd seen the advertisement for a family doctor at Namborra. Of the awakening. Of the emergence from the dark.

'I was in a dark place, too,' Beth said simply. 'And Ron said could we? Dare we? And suddenly it was light again because we dared and we could. And that light...it seemed to flood our lives. Faye, you talk of what I gave Ron but it was two ways. We've loved the locals of Namborra and you guys…you seemed to love us. With Maryanne we seem to have built a medical team to be proud of. More than that, together we rebuilt our lives. We discovered that we dared lots of things. We dared take on the care of this community and you gave it back in spades. With Ron's encouragement—with your encouragement—I even dared have my little boy. Ron gave me my courage back, and that courage spread to all who knew him. You trusted him, you trusted us, and that trust will stay with me to the end.'

She fell silent for a moment, and a hush fell over the hall.

And finally Beth smiled, that tremulous smile that Luc knew and loved.

'To Faye, to all his family, to those who loved him most, I need to say thank you,' she managed. 'Thank you, Ron, from me, from every one of us in Namborra. Thank you for life. Thank you with love.'

And that was it.

The hall erupted, clapping so loudly the roof almost rose. The local bagpiper, a squat little woman with cheeks the colour of beetroot, lifted her pipes and the sound of 'Highland Cathedral' soared to the heavens.

The service was over.

But Beth was still on the stage, staring sightlessly at the departing crowd.

Margie was suddenly lifting the sleeping Toby from Luc's arms.

'Go to her,' she said, almost fiercely. 'If you're her friend…she needs you.'

Did she?

But Luc made his way swiftly up the steps to the stage. Beth was still standing, mute, tears streaming down her face. Farewelling a friend who'd meant so much to her.

He couldn't bear it. Such pain…

He gathered her into him and she folded, crumpling against his chest. He held, he simply held while the world seemed to settle around him.

They needed to step down from the stage. Most people were leaving the hall but a cluster remained, waiting. Luc recognised a few from the day of the crash, Maryanne, some of the nurses, people who'd helped.

Beth's friends?

They were waiting to claim her.

He gave her a moment longer and then gently put her back from him. He produced a handkerchief—he'd had the forethought to bring several—and dried her off.

'People are wanting to talk to you.'

'I… Yes.' She sniffed and blew her nose and mopped up. 'Sorry. I… Where's Toby?'

'Margie has him.' He smiled down at her. 'I think Margie loves him.'

'That's her specialty. Luc…'

'I know.' He met her gaze. This wasn't the time to say it but it had to be said and it had to be said now. 'Beth, we need to regroup. This hurts but I need to say it. While I was sitting down there, watching you, listening to you, I felt such pride…such wonder… But, Beth, what I also thought, what I realised, was that you don't need to marry me. You don't need *me*. You're an amazing woman, a powerhouse of love and talent, and you don't need anyone to give you wings. You've proved that over and over. We might love each other but that's different. I'm taking back my marriage proposal, my love, because the woman I love…she's magnificent just the way she is. She doesn't need me at all.'

She stared up at him, mutely. Seemingly dazed. And then she closed her eyes and seemed to give herself a mental shake.

'I guess…you're right,' she whispered. 'Of course you are. After all, what basis…what basis is love for a marriage?'

'Beth…'

'Don't go on,' she begged. 'You're right, Luc. I learned to be independent once and I can do it again. I don't need marriage. And, no, you're right. I don't need…you.'

Refreshments were served in an adjoining reception hall. Margie took Toby over, setting up an impromptu play area for the littlies in the corner of the hall. Toby was obviously delighted to see his friends. One of the nurses made her way to Beth, pushing a wheelchair, and Beth was able to sink into it and be as she needed to be—the centre of loved attention.

For the locals loved her. Luc could see it, not just in the way so many were waiting their turn to speak to her but in the way so many gazes

gravitated to her. There was community concern and quiet love.

Dr Beth Carmichael had found herself a life in
this community. She was as loved and respected
as Ron had been.

What had she said? One and a half doctors
between the two of them. They'd been so much
more. He could see that.

'She can't come back.' The harsh words came
from behind him. He turned and Maryanne
Clarkson was at his shoulder. This woman was
now Namborra's only doctor and she looked
grim.

He'd been impressed with her the day of the
crash. She'd been unflappable as well as competent. He'd been in the small hospital only briefly
that night, but in the midst of chaos of multiple
injuries he'd noted her triage system, her fast
implementation of rules and the way the staff
moved to her command.

Not a lot of emotion, though, he'd thought,
which was good in an emergency, but now, looking at her grim expression, he thought that same
lack might be a downside.

'Excuse me?' He was balancing a lamington and a mug of tea and watching Beth at the same time. She seemed okay. She was even laughing at something someone had said.

She seemed…at home.

'She can't stay here,' Maryanne told him, following his gaze. 'At least, not to work. I'll tell her if I must, but I gather you're her friend. It might be kinder if you do.'

Beth had already told him she wouldn't be able to work here but he didn't fully understand. 'Why can't she stay here?'

'I can't work with a disabled doctor.'

There was a table behind him. He turned and set down his tea so he could face the middle-aged doctor square on.

'Disabled?'

'She can't see.'

'She can see.'

'Her vision's six/sixty. That's legally blind.'

'Without glasses. With glasses or contact lenses, she's fine.'

'She's not fine. She told me when she applied for the job here. She has trouble distinguishing colour in low light, and if she loses her glasses...' She took a deep breath. 'The day of the crash...look at the victims. Every one of them was over sixty. And Beth was almost there, too. She wouldn't have been able to see grey pillars crumpling. She wouldn't...'

'Have been able to run with a toddler in her arms, all the way out of the car park while the roof caved in almost the instant the plane hit? Neither would you.'

'I would have had a better chance and you know it. It was one thing when we had the two of them backing each other up. Together she and Ron convinced the board they could manage. They did manage,' she conceded, 'but alone she can't and I won't take the risks they both did in covering each other. The hospital's liable if she messes something up.'

She paused and looked across at Beth. 'Look at her now. It'll take months for her to get back on her feet. She's already had to take time off when her child was born and as he's copped normal childhood illnesses. She's had Ron to help her but now... You think I can wear that?'

He was staring at her, stunned by her cold-ness. 'For a competent colleague. For a friend? Yes, I can. Bad things happen to all of us, Dr Clarkson.'

'Yes, and colleagues support when support's needed,' Maryanne snapped. 'Until whoever it is accepts their limitations are long term and chooses a more suitable role. Which isn't here. I was against hiring the pair of them, and look at them now. One's dead and one's even more disabled than when she started.'

'That's not their fault.'

'And it's not my fault either and it's not going to be. I can't spend my time worrying about her.'

'You don't have a choice. She's been cleared by the medical board as fit for practice. How many employment laws are you breaking?'

'I'm not breaking any. I'm simply saying I can't work with her, so if she chooses to return she'll be on her own. You think she can cope, with the load she's carrying?' She gave a grim nod as if the conversation was ended, as indeed it was. 'So there it is. Tell her she needs to look elsewhere for a less demanding job. You tell her—or I will.'

* * *

Then came another medical crisis, only not one he had to deal with. The head of the outback clinic was on the phone before he'd recovered his tea—and his equilibrium. 'Mate, there's been a car crash here. We'll be sending the chopper straight to Sydney so we can't pick you up this afternoon.'

'That's okay.' He'd already factored this into his plans. A commercial flight, small but reliable, left every day at midday so they could stay in Beth's apartment overnight.

And then he thought… Beth's apartment was a hospital apartment.

It wouldn't be hers for much longer.

And he watched her face as she talked on to the locals. He saw the rigid set of her smile as she was asked how long it would be before she was back for good, and he thought, She already knows it. She knows Maryanne, she's worked with her for years so she'll know exactly what she's thinking. Maryanne was a competent doctor who wouldn't bend the rules one bit, constantly looking over her shoulder for the bogie man of legal liability. For Beth she must be a nightmare.

Beth was starting to look exhausted. He headed over and told her what was happening with the plane, and she reacted almost with relief. It meant she could have time out in her apartment, rest—have space to come to terms with her lack of future here?

But first she needed to field invitations as the locals realised she was staying.

'Sorry, guys.' She was back on her crutches while Luc held a very sleepy Toby. 'I…' She glanced uncertainly at Luc. 'We need a quiet night.'

'How long do you think before you'll be back for good?' Margie asked directly, and Beth hesitated just a moment too long.

But then she managed a smile and he watched her shoulders brace. Moving on.

'Who knows how long this leg needs to heal?' she said lightly. 'I'll let you know.'

She gave Luc a bright smile that said clearly— Rescue me—and ten minutes later they were back in Beth's cosy little apartment. Beth was putting Toby into his cot, reuniting him with toys he'd been missing, while Luc was pacing the apartment, wanting to punch something.

The anger stayed—but with it came confusion.

Sometime during the service things had cleared for him. Now...fog was creeping back.

Beth headed for the fridge and poured wine for herself, offered him a beer, settled thankfully into a massive armchair and surveyed him thoughtfully. Even with the broken leg she was a woman in charge of her domain, he thought.

Except she wasn't, and it needed to be talked of. But first...the biggie. 'Beth...what I said at the service...about marriage...'

'Luc, that's over.' She met his gaze, calmly, almost challengingly. 'It should never have resurfaced as an option. It only did because Toby was ill and neither of us were thinking. You don't want to be married to me.'

Confusion deepened. Of course he wanted to be married to this amazing woman, but to hold her back...

How to say this? How to explain what he felt?

And what did he feel? How could he move forward from here? There were so many conflicting emotions.

'Beth, I don't want you to have to accept that you need me. Because I'm looking at you now...'

'Yeah, folded into an armchair because I've been tottering about on a broken leg...'

'That's not what I mean. Beth, somehow you've turned into someone amazing. Only maybe that's not true. I'm starting to think you've been amazing all along.' He was struggling here, trying to see inside him. Trying to sort fact from emotion.

'I know I coddled you but you flew the coop and, hey, you knew how to fly all along. You're a competent, practising doctor. You're a great mum. The locals here clearly adore you. With or without Ron, you've made a success of your life. Today...when you stood up and talked about Ron there wasn't a dry eye in the house but it wasn't just about Ron. It was about you. Until one tragic plane crash, you had your life under control and it will be again.'

She didn't respond. She met his gaze, her chin slightly tilted. Defiant?

How hard was all this to work out? How hard was it to say? But somehow he forced himself to continue. 'Beth, I would care for you,' he told her. 'I know that about myself. But I also know I'll risk smothering you, and maybe Toby, too. And I get it. I talked to Maryanne after the service and she's told me how she can't accept your disabilities. She's one cold woman. There's a part of me that wants to really tell her what I think of her, but there's another part of me that wants to agree with her because all I want to do is take you back to Sydney and keep you in cotton wool. Which...' He took a deep breath. 'Which is not what you want. During the awfulness of the past weeks it might be what you've thought you needed but it's not true into the future. Is it?'

'No.' Beth's expression was still calm. Assessing. Watching how he was feeling rather than thinking about herself? 'You're right, Luc. For now... Who knows what I'll do, but remarrying... I know I said maybe, but you're right, I said it for the wrong reasons. It feels like admitting defeat. When Toby was ill that was how I felt, defeated, but now...' She braced herself and tried to smile. 'Wherever I go, I don't need care twenty-four seven. You've been wonderful, Luc, as you've been in the past, but I don't need… constant wonderful. I can't keep needing.'

He was right, then. The thought gave him no joy.

This morning he'd accompanied Beth to Namborra and it had felt right. By some miracle Toby and Beth had been his to protect.

So what had changed? What was making him step back now?

It was because he loved her.

And he got it. In that one blinding moment of clarity, when she'd been on the stage, when she'd been talking to a community who loved her, he'd seen it.

She was wonderful, his Beth—except she wasn't *his* because she didn't need the restrictions he was bound to place on her life.

And she was smiling at him now, mistily, emotion front and centre, but he knew the smile said that he was right. The last weeks had thrown them back to a place that hadn't suited either of them.

'Can I help you fight to stay here? Can we face down Maryanne together? She's well out of order.' He was struggling to find his voice and practicalities seemed the only way to go.

Once again, asking her to need him?

But she shook her head. 'It's not possible. I thought of it when Ron had the flu last year and we faced the fact that he'd have to retire eventually.' She still had her voice under control, but her eyes were a different matter. They were bright with unshed tears.

'Maryanne's seen my medical records—she actually accessed my past hospital records without asking, but that's another story. She's adamant I'm a risk. We had a car crash here a few months back—a nasty one. I had to crawl under and put in an IV line while the guys were stabilising the site. I cut myself on the way out, quite deep. Maryanne had to stitch me and she spent the entire time she stitched telling me the board couldn't be responsible for my stupidity. The fact that the kid survived because of the line I put in, and anyone else going under there would have been under the same risk as I was, was irrelevant. But she's threatened… If Ron's not here to work—as my guide dog, that's what she called him—she's said she'll leave.'

'Of all the vicious…'

'It's not vicious. It's pragmatic. She'll walk because she can't accept the responsibility.'

'Sort of like the opposite of me,' he said ruefully, and she managed a smile.

'I guess. You need to be needed and Maryanne runs a mile. Or she makes me run a mile. Maryanne's competent, hard working and she doesn't have a child. She's a much better bet for the town than I am.'

'So the town's stuck with one doctor instead of two.'

'It'd be one and a half…'

'You're a whole lot more than half a doctor,' he growled, and she even managed a chuckle.

'Yeah, but you're biased.'

'Because I love you.'

'As a friend, Luc,' she said softly. 'Please, from now on, that's what it has to be.'

And he thought of what that meant. Tonight. Sleeping on the couch instead of holding Beth's body. The sensation of loss was almost overwhelming.

'Yeah, it sucks,' she said, and he could see she

knew what he was thinking. 'But it's the only way, Luc.'

'I could…try to back off.'

'And pigs could learn to fly.' She sighed, her face bleak. 'Luc, I need a rest. Would you mind…maybe wandering down to the supermarket and buying a couple of steaks for dinner? The pub will be packed with locals tonight and I don't want to face them. I'll come back here in a few weeks, when I've finished rehab, so I can pack up and say my goodbyes properly. But for the town, tonight should be all about those we lost, not about me.'

'They're losing you, too. And so am I.' The desolation he felt was almost overwhelming.

'Yeah, but the alternative is me losing me,' she said, striving for lightness. 'And that's a whole heap worse.'

He headed off on his steak quest. Beth lay on the bed she'd slept in for the last few years and waited for exhaustion to do its job. To send her into oblivion for a couple of hours. She ached for time out.

It didn't happen.

What had she done?

And where was her future?

It wasn't here, in this cosy apartment she'd called home for the past few years.

She'd made herself a life here. She'd worked professionally, she'd had her baby and she'd felt a part of this community. But a part of her had always known it had to end. Ron had been nearing the point of retirement and Maryanne was a fixture. She and Ron had even joked about it— making an advertisement for a Ron replacement.

'Wanted, three quarters of a doctor to hold up another three quarters of a doctor.'

'Yeah, but we've been more than that,' she muttered into the stillness. She and Ron had been an awesome team.

Grief was all around her, grief for Ron, the gentle, kindly man she'd called a friend for so long, grief that her time here was over…and grief, all over again, for a man called Luc.

'I should never have slept with him,' she muttered. 'It's made it so much worse.

'It couldn't be any worse.' She was answering herself. 'You've never fallen out of love with him. Couldn't you just…learn to be dependent again? Let him take control?'

But she knew she couldn't.

She imagined Toby, climbing trees, falling off skateboards, doing all the dumb things kids did as they grew. Would Luc let him take risks that all children had to take in order to turn into independent people?

'It'll never happen.' She knew it but it didn't make her decision less bleak. She took off her glasses and let the world blur.

'I can move on,' she muttered. 'I've done it before and I'll do it again.'

But if she let herself need Luc… How much easier…

'Not going to happen,' she said grimly into the silence, and she knew those four words were the final verdict.

CHAPTER NINE

'So, YOU AND LUC...'

'Friends. Only friends.'

Rehab at Bondi Bayside was intense. There was little time for chat among those fighting to recover what they'd lost, or those learning to make the most of their new norms. Beth and Harriet fitted into a camp apiece. Beth's leg was likely to recover to full use but Harriet was facing a lifetime of weakness.

This morning Harriet and Beth found themselves on the mats together, soft balls between their knees, raising their legs over and over.

Beth was getting better every day. Harriet was struggling.

If anyone else had asked personal questions Beth would have shrugged them off, but Harriet had become a friend. And maybe Harriet was facing long-term issues that almost mirrored Beth's.

'It must be strange, living with your ex-husband.' Harriet was probing gently but Beth glanced across at her and saw the set of her face, the lines of entrenched pain as she raised and lowered her injured leg, and knew she was using Beth's story to deflect thinking of what was starting to be obvious. That the damage to Harriet's leg was permanent.

She knew by now that Harriet's depression was bone deep. Coming to terms with disability…it sucked.

There was little Beth could do to help her but she could at least answer honestly.

'It is weird,' she admitted. 'What's between Luc and I…it's been so intense it's hard to step back, but we're both trying.' She tried for a smile. 'He's too good a friend to lose.'

'He is that,' Harriet said. 'The whole team… they're lovely. But if anything happened… between me and Pete… I don't think we could ever be just friends.'

'Yeah?' Beth had her own views on Pete, aided by Luc's harsh summary.

'Pete's lightweight. Harriet's fallen hard but I can't see Pete sticking round for the long haul.

Where is he now? She's injured and he's not exactly playing the devoted spouse.'

'Maybe Harriet doesn't need him...like you assume need,' she'd suggested, but he'd snorted.

'I'm hearing rumours and they're not pretty. I wish she could find someone else...'

Maybe Harriet and Luc, Beth thought as she pushed her ball up and winced as unused muscles screamed their protest. But for some reason... The thought made her feel ill.

So much for just being friends.

She had to get her ankle back to normal and get herself out of here. Make herself a new life.

Learn again to be independent.

He's too good a friend to lose...

He was that, she thought, but the atmosphere in the apartment now... Aagh!

'So what do you do at night?' Harriet asked into the suddenly loaded silence.

And that led to even more loaded silence.

We spend the night concentrating on not jumping each other. That was the honest answer but she could hardly go there. What happened was usually an early dinner, a trip to the beach, time playing with Toby on the sand...pretending they weren't a family? And then home. No. Back to Luc's apartment, not home, she told herself fiercely. And she'd say she was tired and head to bed. She'd lie in the spare bedroom beside Toby's cot and listen to Toby snuffle in his sleep and try not to think about Luc in the next room.

Sometimes Luc was called out to work and then it was easier. Or almost easier because then she kept thinking of what he was doing, putting himself in harm's way. That didn't lead to sleep either.

All in all...friend or not, it would be easier if she was staying somewhere else, she thought, but how would Luc feel if she rejected even that much of his friendship?

'Hard, isn't it?' Harriet said sympathetically.

And Beth thought, I've been silent for too long and she knows. She guesses...

'Yeah, well...'

'It probably is worth fighting to stay friends, though.'

Harriet's voice had turned thoughtful. Beth figured she was using this to distract her from her own problems, so that was okay. She should even encourage it.

Except talking about it was hard.

Even thinking about it was doing her head in.

'How about gaming?' Harriet asked into the stillness.

And Beth thought, *What?*

'Um…gaming?'

'Mystic Killers,' Harriet said. 'It's an online game. Sam…you've met Sam? She's one of the other nurses on SDR and she's pretty much my bestie. She's been researching stuff that might help me kill time, and Mystic Killers does seem to work. Turns out swatting dragons can get rid of a whole heap of angst. Off with their heads. You need to watch the fire spouts, though. And the babies.'

'Really?' She said it with such caution that Harriet smiled.

'Oh, yeah. The ones with forked tongues are the worst. Sam's set me up as Sneak-Swiper and I'm getting better at dodging. It beats lying in bed thinking about what I'm about to do with the rest of my life. Hey, another ten push-ups of this dumb ball and we're out of here. You, too? Do you have time before picking up Toby to learn to play?'

'I...guess. But my eyes... Harriet, I can't...'

'Oh, Beth,' Harriet said, instantly appalled. 'I'm so sorry. I didn't think. I should have...'

'It's okay.' She managed a smile across at her friend. 'That's something I've learned not to flinch at.' She hesitated and then looked at Harriet, at the mess that was still her leg. Did she know her well enough now to say it like it was?

Why not? She'd had enough people tiptoeing around her when her sight had gone, assuming the worst. Luc, front and centre.

'I'm thinking that might be something you need to face in the future, too, now,' she told her. 'A lifetime of people questioning whether you're up to things. Sometimes it's concern and care. Sometimes it's not, it's downright patronising, but if you look for patronising you'll spend the rest of your life defensive.'

'Yeah,' Harriet said grimly. 'I see that. So Luc...concern and care?

'You'd better believe it.'

'And patronising?'

'He doesn't quite get the distinction but he tries.'

'But not hard enough.'

'I don't think he can try any harder,' Beth said bluntly. 'And I have no idea how he can do any better. But that's okay. Another couple of weeks and he can stop trying again. We'll go back to being...'

'Friends?'

'I hope so,' she whispered, and then pushed herself together. 'But gaming...what is this Mystic Killers?'

'Something to play at night if you can't...play at night. And something to vent a little frustration on. Or a lot. But if you can't...'

'I'm not good with fast objects on small screens.'

'But maybe...' Harriet paused for thought and then grinned. 'Hey, there's an enormous screen in the health education unit on the top floor.' She hauled her hospital ID out of the top pocket of her gym gear. 'They hardly use it and I'm officially allowed access. Do you have a big telly at home?'

'I... Yes. Back at Namborra.' Or wherever she ended up.

'There you go, then. Learn here and you'll fly.

Okay, Beth, hold onto your hat, I'm about to introduce you to a whole new world.'

There'd been a minor crisis in the outer suburbs but it was very minor. A recycling warehouse had caught fire. It had produced a frightening amount of flames and smoke, the authorities had panicked and pulled in the big guns, but the team came back to Bondi in a chopper with no patients. There'd been no casualties apart from a bit of smoke inhalation. The local medics had it under control.

It meant, though, that Luc had missed his time at the beach with Toby and Beth, and he'd definitely missed it. It was now almost nine, the time when Beth usually said goodnight, headed into the spare room with Toby and closed the door behind her.

She might already have the door closed.

He had to get used to it. Another couple of weeks and she'd be done with rehab and out of here, he thought, as he rode the elevator to his apartment. It was the way things were, the sensible option.

But he didn't feel sensible. He felt frustrated.

He had so few nights left and he'd just missed one. He put his key in the lock and felt tension tighten across his forehead. Please let her still be awake...

He opened the door—and stopped short.

She *was* still awake. She was wearing the soft, blue jogging suit she wore for rehab. Her hair was tousled, she was nestled under a rug on the sofa with her braced leg on a chair in front of her, she was wearing headphones and she was...

Staring at the world's biggest television. It took up almost the entire wall unit.

There were dragons on the screen. Large dragons. As he stared, one lunged forward, all fangs and fire, so real, so vast he almost backed out of the door.

Beth's hand rose on the controller and the dragon exploded into a thousand gory pieces, sliding down the screen and disappearing into the ether.

'Got him! Awesome! He fell right into my trap.' She glanced around at Luc and her grin almost split her face. 'That's Slime Vader taken care of. Let's see what else they can throw at me. Let 'em come. I'm ready.' She typed something fast on the screen and then put the remote aside. 'They can regroup for a while, not that it'll do 'em any good. Sneak-Swiper's in control.' And then she turned her grin to him. 'Hi, dear. How was your day?'

He…blinked. A domestic scene…the little wife bearing slippers and domestic harmony… Not so much.

'Dragons,' he tried, cautiously.

'Mystic Killers,' she said, as if that explained everything. 'Sneak-Swiper and I are on a mission. You want to join us?'

'Sneak-Swiper?'

'That'd be Harriet. She doesn't seem to enjoy it as much as me—she's not bloodthirsty enough—but she's more skilled and I'm improving every minute. Did you see the end of Slime Vader? I'm Mouse-Who-Roared, by the way. That's intentional. Everyone knows dragons are scared of mice.'

'I… Of course.' He ventured a little further into the room and looked around with caution. 'Um…my telly? My sound system?'

'I didn't trade them in, if that's what you're thinking,' she said, and chuckled, and the sound of her laugh was a shock. It was warm and deep and true. It was a sound he hadn't heard…for years?

It made him think…

Don't think.

'They're safely stowed under my bed,' she assured him as if that was entirely sensible. 'With my rubbish eyesight, I couldn't game using your set.'

'So you bought a new one?'

'Hey, I'm sensible.' She stood up and wobbled and reached for her crutches. He didn't step forward and steady her. It almost killed him not to.

'I have a perfectly perfect big telly back in Namborra,' she continued, happily. 'This baby is from the rental place that supplies the hospital. They were a bit stunned when I told them the size I needed but happy to oblige in the end. The console's new, though, bought for me this afternoon by Pete. Harriet's boyfriend?' Her smile slipped a bit then.

'Luc, do you know what the deal is there? I'm starting to have serious reservations about that relationship and I so don't want Harry to get hurt. Harriet was aching for his visit—I could see her face light up with hope every time the door opened. Then when he did arrive… I went to leave but before I could, she asked him if he'd organise me the console. And Pete was out of there so fast… It was like he was aching for an excuse to get out, even though he'd just arrived. Then he insisted on playing here with me when I knew she wanted him. So here he was, looking after the little woman, only it was me and not Harriet who was the little woman. It was nice of him to do it but really…what does she see in him?'

Pete…

There was so much going on here it was making his head spin.

Pete was a firefighter, one of Kev's crew. He and Harriet had been an item for a year now but Luc, too, had reservations. The guy seemed all testosterone-driven ego.

And that he'd been here with Beth… The tension he'd been feeling in the elevator escalated.

'So…is he a toe-rag or am I just imagining it?' Beth was apparently not noticing his…anger?

'As far as I know he hasn't played away.' He tried to haul his mind away from Beth's flushed face and tousled hair, from the cuteness of her jogging suit, from…well, just from Beth. Focus on Harriet, he told himself, and tried. Harriet and Pete. 'My concerns are only instinct.' He sighed. 'With her injuries, I hope I'm wrong. She needs him.'

'Need's not a basis for a relationship,' she snapped, and he flinched. There it was, the underlying reason why he couldn't have this woman. Because she refused to concede…need?

Because he couldn't come to terms with what she really needed. Which was independence.

'Want to play?' she asked, moving on fast, as if she guessed the tensions simmering underneath.

'Play?'

'Mystic Killers,' she said with all the patience in the world. 'I was getting hammered when you arrived. Yeah, I blew up Slime Vader, but there's bigger, scarier dragons in the background. I could use someone at my back. Hey, there's a role that might suit. I need you, Luc Braxton, to kill my dragons. You ever tinkered with online gaming?'

'No,' he said faintly.

'Well, seeing your entire apartment has been

taken over, maybe it's time for you to learn. You need a handle. How about…?' She paused and considered. 'Protect-Or-Die.'

'Die…'

'Nobility is your middle name. You don't have a suit of armour in your apartment by any chance? Sword? Chain mail?'

'Um…no.'

'Then we'll just have to use our imagination. Want to share my rug instead? Come on. I need you.' And she tossed back a corner of the fluffy rug someone from Namborra had sent her as a get-well gift and invited him in.

She needed him.

She didn't.

He stood and gazed at her and she beamed back. There wasn't a single sexy nuance in the way she was holding the rug. She was all bounce and excitement. *Let's go slay some dragons together…*

She'd moved on, he thought. That week of clinging, of need, was over. She'd figured it out. From now he was only a friend. But she was offering friendship. On her terms. Her telly. Her hired console. Her rug.

Take it or leave it, her smile was saying, and what choice did he have?

'Give me a minute to find myself a beer and haul my boots off,' he told her. 'How many dragons do we need to kill?'

There was something about blowing fire-breathing dragons into a thousand unidentifiable body parts that settled things inside her—especially when she was blowing things up with Luc snuggled beside her.

He got the gist of the game in minutes, but he played differently from Harriet, or from Pete who'd played for a while supposedly to make sure the set worked. Pete blasted his way in front and ended up pretty much dead for his pains, over and over. She and Harriet played as a team, stalking Mystic World with steady purpose and a certain amount of caution.

Luc played tactical right from the beginning. He slipped in behind her, covering her back. For a start she thought he was content to stay back until he'd learned the fundamentals of the game, but as the night wore on he still stayed back.

And she grew bolder because of it. She found

she was moving faster, surer, knowing as each threat emerged she had a solid, safe presence backing her up. When she missed her aim, Luc was there, blasting her way out of trouble. Steady. Intent. Watchful.

But also having a heap of fun. When she hesitated, knowing just over the rise there'd be dragons of truly epic proportions, he was egging her on.

'Go, girl. You can handle hot. Besides, I just won us enough points for you to rise from the dead twice. I wish we had this set up in ER. How about that for a medical scenario? They bring in a crash victim, I go kill a couple of dragons, get my Rise-From-The-Dead points and all's well with the world. And yet they never taught this at med school. Okay, Mouse-Who-Roared. Go!'

And she did, storming the mighty Mystic Gate, sword flashing, fire on all sides, magic and mayhem scattering before her. Luc followed behind, neutralised threats, egged her on, giving her courage. Cheered as she blew things up that needed blowing up. Handed over his points to save her when she was devoured. Joined her in inescapable laughter as they stormed the tower and took on five dragons and their world blew up and they were blasted from the top of the tower, with only Luc's points to save them.

Then Beth headed over a rise and spotted a dragon's nest, complete with adorable-looking, doe-eyed baby dragons. The babies were pecking their way out of their shells and staggering into their new world. Cute as...

She turned her Mystic Blaster to the nest and shot them all into the middle of next week. Leaving Luc...hornswoggled.

'You shot babies,' Luc said blankly.

'Kill or be killed.' She grinned. 'That's twenty less threats we need to face before we gain the Mystic Throne. Besides, grown up they'll threaten our world and I'm all for protecting our world. We're a team, Luc Braxton. Get a grip.'

And then another giant loomed behind them and ethical questions faded. Apparently, you had to pay—a lot—for decimating dragon nests.

Uh-oh. There weren't enough points left in anyone's bank to save them from what happened next.

'We need better tactics,' Luc said, as their online bodies lay crumpled on the dusty plains, with the Mystic Kingdom a mere speck on the horizon. 'I think your sword arm needs a broader sweep. And maybe babies are a no go.'

'The babies need thought,' she conceded. 'Maybe we need to let 'em leave the nest and grow fangs before we pick 'em off. Next time you win points, how about using them for that, rather than all this noble point-saving so you can heal me.'

'I don't like to see you dead.'

'Hey, we survive dead to fight another day. Look at us.'

'Yeah, zero points and back where we started.' He sighed and then cheered up. 'Want to try again?'

'Sorry. Time for a bacon sandwich and bed. Toby'll be up at dawn and he won't take drag-ons as an excuse.' She tossed back her rug and pushed herself clumsily to her feet. 'But a re-match is certainly in order. Tomorrow night? I reckon in two weeks we could be quite a team.'

'Two weeks.'

'That's when I go.' She shrugged and smiled. 'Back to Namborra for a start, and then back to Brisbane. I've decided. You know Mum and

Dad still own an apartment there? It's empty at the moment so Toby and I will stay there until we figure what to do.'

So she had things arranged.

Two weeks. Right.

The emptiness, the desolation, was suddenly so great it threatened to overwhelm him.

He watched as she struggled over to the kitchenette, as she set about making toasted sandwiches.

He should do it for her, or at least offer to help, but he knew by now that she'd shrug him away.

I can do it.

She could, he thought. She didn't need him.

The thought was breaking him in two.

We're a team, Luc Braxton.

Not so much.

He thought of the last couple of hours, of Beth assessing the dragon nest and blasting it into oblivion. The Beth he'd known—or thought he'd known—would have flinched. Killing cute baby dragons? That wasn't for the soft-hearted.

What had she said?

I'm all for protecting our world.

But he was the protector.

He watched her cook for him and he felt like his worlds were somehow colliding. The impact was smashing something and he wasn't sure what.

He should get up, insist on helping, force her to sit while he cooked.

Or he should relax while she cooked, be grateful that she was happy and helping him.

Neither felt right.

His background was all around him, the need to stay within himself, to be self-contained, to protect, to not need anyone.

He watched her struggle to get to the refrigerator and it almost killed him to let her cope on her own.

But he had to. She didn't want him. She didn't need him. She and Toby would move back to Brisbane and get on with their lives while he went on saving people. Doing what he was good at.

Beth was okay at saving people, too, he conceded. She was skilled, level-headed, practical… and had she really blasted those dragon babies to save the world?

Yes, she had. She was practical.

He wouldn't be so good at living with a practical partner, he conceded. A partner who resented him stepping in. Caring.

So therefore...

'Toastie,' she said, and handed over a plate loaded with buttery, oozy calories. 'And then bed for me, and maybe for you, too? I know you, Luc Braxton. You've been out there saving the world, having quite a day.'

'While you've saved Mystic World.'

'Not yet I haven't,' she said serenely. 'But I will. Tomorrow or the next day or the day after that. And then...there's lots more worlds to save and I'll find some other way to save them than by being a family doctor in Namborra. So don't you worry about me.' She fetched her own toastie from the fry-pan, waved it a couple of times until it cooled and then held it like she was proposing a toast. 'Here's to a future without threats,' she said. 'Here's to the saviours of Mystic World, and dragon exterminators extraordinaire. And here's to you, Luc, exterminating all other threats. We make a great team, you know. It's just...we need to save our worlds separately.'

* * *

But an hour later... It was all very well to say that sort of thing to Luc's face, Beth conceded. It was quite another to lie in the dark and think it.

Saving the world separately...

Oh, she still loved him.

She should never have slept with him again, she thought bleakly. It'd brought it all back.

'But it was back already,' she said into the dark. 'It never went away.'

'It has to go away. I have no use for it.'

What?

Love?

Did she still love him?

That was a no-brainer. Of course she did.

She thought of him, playing the game, protecting her back.

'I could do the same for him,' she muttered into the dark. 'We could do the same for each other. Watch each other's backs. Be in each other's corners.'

But it wouldn't be like that. She'd watched him surreptitiously as she'd made their toasties and she'd seen the strain letting her do such a simple task had imposed on him. It'd almost kill him to let her take normal, everyday risks, she thought, and he'd do the same for Toby. He'd wrap them in care, and they'd stifle.

She thought of Harriet with her Pete, Pete who couldn't bear to care. Pete who needed his Harriet to be perfect or he couldn't cope.

'So we have the opposite.' She buried her face in her pillow. Her leg was aching. She should get up and take painkillers but in a sense the pain in her leg was distracting her from the pain in her heart.

She couldn't live with him.

She loved him.

She had to leave.

And in the next room Luc was struggling with demons of his own.

She was going to leave, but how the hell would she cope without him?

Easily.

She had a gammy leg and weak eyesight but neither of those things made her need him. He had no place in her life.

But he wanted her.

So step back, he told himself. Do what he'd done tonight, protect from the rear, let her lead.

Except…did she even want him to do that? He was starting to figure it out. Even tonight when they had been playing…any minute he'd been expecting her to turn on him and tell him to go find his own dragons.

He'd been hunting his own dragons for years now. That was what his job was all about. He'd saved Beth this time. He'd helped her but she no longer needed him so it was back to doing what he always did. Holding himself solitary, unattached, ready to fight whatever needed to be fought and then move on.

But in the next room… Beth and Toby…

They were doing his head in.

He ached for them to need him.

He needed them to need him.

And there was a thought he couldn't get his head around. He had no way of interpreting it.

All he knew was that Beth was right. Being with her when she didn't need him would drive him into a place he couldn't fathom. He had no choice. If he loved her…and he did love her, he knew enough of his head now to accept that fact as irreversible...then he had to let her fly on her own.

He had to let her go.

CHAPTER TEN

BRISBANE WAS BORING.

There were job opportunities—of course there were. She was a qualified doctor with solid experience. Very few employers took the same view of her sight limitations as Maryanne. She was qualified, she wasn't an obvious loose cannon, therefore she was employable. But her leg still needed work. She was still hobbling, still having trouble carrying Toby.

Maybe she should have stayed at Luc's for a while longer, accepted his help, accepted the help of the lovely grandmotherly Alice.

Except she had her pride.

And her fear.

Yeah, okay, she'd been terrified at how close she was growing to Luc. She was terrified she'd become the woman he wanted her to be, a woman who loved and depended on him.

Depended... Yeah, that was the cut. As soon

as the rehab doctors had told her she was free to work on her own, she'd run. She'd had no choice.

She'd flown back to Namborra before she'd come to Brisbane. She and Toby had spent a few days catching up with friends and packing up her apartment.

She'd sort of hoped Maryanne might change her mind but it wasn't going to happen. Maryanne seemed tired, overwrought and stressed to the limit as she coped with the workload of three doctors, but it had taken only one short conversation for Beth to realise she wasn't backing down.

'Yes, I'm stressed but do you think having to watch over your shoulder to make sure you're not stuffing things up will make things better?'

She'd tried, for what was to be the last time. 'Maryanne, my sight's not a problem. Not if you...'

'That's just it. Not if I cover for you. It's not going to happen, Dr Carmichael. If Ron had been able to move faster to get out of the way...if you'd been able to see those pillars crumbling...'

'You know that's unfair.'

'Unfair or not, I'm not about to risk a medical negligence suit on my watch.'

There was nothing more to be said. She'd said her goodbyes and left.

Which left her in her parents' elegant apartment overlooking the Brisbane river, working on her rehab, playing with Toby, trying to figure what to do with her life.

She didn't want to be a shift doctor in a city clinic.

She wanted the country. She wanted Luc.

She needed…

No. She wasn't sure what she needed. All she knew was that she didn't need Luc enough to run back to him.

She'd brought Mystic Killers with her. Dragon slaying was good for the quiet times.

When in doubt, kill…

When in doubt, slay dragons.

Luc had set his own screen up again, and gone out and bought his own gaming console, as Beth's huge screen had gone back to the rental agency and she'd taken her console with her. He played online with Harriet and Sam.

'You know, you can still play online with Beth,' Harriet told him but the idea seemed…

Hard?

Yeah, like watching her limp away hadn't been the hardest thing he'd ever done in his life.

She didn't need him. She was out there slaying dragons all by herself and that was the way she wanted it.

He just had to accept it.

Two weeks. Three weeks. Four.

He was going nuts. He needed catastrophes. Disasters. Anything to make the pain go away.

'You love her.' He was sitting on the end of Harriet's bed—yet again. Harriet seemed almost as morose as he was. Almost? That was crazy all by itself. She had so much more to be miserable about. Her leg was taking its own sweet time to heal, the doctors were unsure if she'd ever regain full strength and on top of that Pete was avoiding her. Toerag. Hell, if Beth needed him like Harriet needed Pete, Luc thought, then… then things would be okay.

He wanted to punch Pete.

He wanted to punch…dragons.

He wanted Beth.

A month. Time to organise crèche. Time to take a job.

So what if the only jobs available seemed to be working sessional clinics? She could handle that. As long as she didn't try to work in poor light she was fine, and it wasn't as if most sessional doctors did house calls.

She found a good crèche for Toby. It wasn't as friendly as the Namborra childcare but it was the best she could do.

She started working four mornings a week, working on her leg for the rest of the time. And playing with Toby.

Thank heaven for Toby. He kept her sane. He kept her happy.

Almost…

The call came at three in the morning. The worst ones did, Luc thought as he groped in the dark for the phone. He was used to it, though. He was wide awake, reaching for his clothes as he listened.

'A crash on the cliffs north of Illawarra.' Mabel was wasting no words. Like Luc, she'd have been pulled from sleep and the adrenaline would have coursed straight in. 'An eighteen-wheeler, one of those huge double trucks. The driver's lost control for some reason. He's crashed through the barriers and into oncoming traffic. He's okay but a car's been pushed down the cliff. It's hanging by nothing just above the sea. As far as we can tell, there's a woman and three kids inside, too terrified to move. A couple of locals are trying to abseil down to stabilise the car but there's fog and wind. Two minutes to get to the chopper, Luc. Minimum crew as you'll want the chopper for transfer. I'll send backup after you. Gina's heading for the roof now. Chopper's ready. You, Blake, Samantha. Go.'

He went.

She'd seen ten patients that morning and almost all had been boring.

That wasn't exactly a kind thing to think, she conceded as she tried to sleep that night, but walk-in clinics tended to attract boring.

If people had something they were really worried about, they tended to take time off work and make an appointment with their family doctor. If something was urgent, then they'd head to their nearest hospital. Beth's clinic got the rest.

Today Beth had handled five requests for certificates from office workers who'd had to take time off work because of minor ailments. A teenager wanting birth control who didn't want to face the same family doctor her mum used. A construction worker with an annoying rash—wearing polyester while digging in the heat wasn't the wisest move. A young mum who'd popped in on impulse because her baby was having trouble feeding. The last had at least had been rewarding as Beth had recognised underlying postnatal depression, though the head of the clinic had been less than impressed when he'd seen Beth's timesheet for the consultation.

There'd also been two hopefuls who'd seen a new name on the medical list and thought they'd try her as an easy mark for drugs.

It wasn't exactly satisfying medicine.

At least she'd picked the postnatal depression, she told herself. Left untreated it could have led to disaster, so she had done some good. But this couldn't sustain her long term. She wanted to be a family doctor, someone people chose when they had real problems. She wanted to be a doctor who saw mothers through pregnancies and picked postnatal depression before it did real damage.

'You're lucky to have any job right now,' she said into the dark, and she knew she was. She'd fought desperately hard to qualify as a doctor. And, yes, her time at Namborra had been fantastic but she'd been lucky.

'You make your own luck,' she muttered, and wondered how on earth she was going to make her own luck now.

'So one step at a time,' she told herself. 'Get your leg better.'

And stop thinking about Luc?

Where was he now?

'Out caring for the world,' she said out loud. 'Out setting the world to rights.'

'I could help him.'

'As if he'd ever let you... Get real.'

The car had been hit head on, and then propelled mercilessly over the cliff, the force of the truck smashing it through the metal barricade to plunge almost thirty feet down the cliff.

It hung, seemingly by a wing and a prayer, ten feet above the waves.

The cliff was almost concave, the rock face scooping inward then out to form a slight ledge. The ledge had caught the car—just. It was wedged precariously, its front fender on the ledge, the rest of it seemingly a crumpled wreck.

By the time the chopper landed on the clifftop, the local coastguard boat was in view, beavering through rough seas, heading for the base of the cliff, but the rocks underneath would allow no approach by sea. The night was windy and wild. Gina was having trouble even steadying the chopper to land.

The coastguard's searchlights lit the scene like day as they did their initial assessment but there was no way a boat could get near.

An ambulance was parked on the clifftop, and a couple of paramedics caring for someone they assumed was the truck driver. Minor lacerations and shock, they'd been told. There was also a fire engine, plus about six other cars. There were guys on the cliff face dressed in hard hats, with ropes looped around their shoulders. Local abseilers called on to help? They weren't going over, though. Amateurs?

This wasn't the scene for amateurs, Luc thought, and thanked God they'd had the sense to wait. The look of that cliff… If they'd tried to get down there they might well become further casualties.

There was a moment's silence between those in the chopper as they all stared down at the car. The ledge it was on was so narrow. They could almost see it teetering. 'How many did Mabel say?' Blake asked at last, and his voice was almost a whisper through the headphones. They'd pull themselves together before they landed, but right now the initial reaction from all of them was horror.

'Woman and three kids,' Luc said. His headset was connected to base. 'Mabel's just radioed in what we know. The driver's a Tess McKnight, thirty-four. Kids are Zoe, eight, Tom, six, and Robbie, three.'

'What the hell were they doing out here at this time of night?' Blake muttered.

And Luc knew that, too. 'Anniversary party

in Sydney. Driving home late. Husband's following behind, driving Gran and Grandpa and Aunty. He's on the cliff.'

That led to further silence. Scenes like this were appalling but the addition of family watching on…it added tension to tension. The team would need to turn off distress, turn off emotion if they were to have any hope of rescuing anyone.

'Mabel says the firies have called in cranes,' Luc said into the headphones. 'Two, due here any minute. If we can get cables to the car we'll have something to attach them to. She's telling me the boys with ropes are part of a local abseiling group but the cliffs here are sandstone and they don't like their chances.'

'Right.' A moment's further thought while Blake assessed and came to a decision. 'Sam, you're up top,' Blake told her. 'I know you have the skills but you don't have the experience. Luc, you and I head down. Cables, hooks…take thin lines and Sam'll guide down what we need when we reach the car.' The chopper was settling now. They could no longer see the car dangling over the ocean, but the vision was seared into the minds of them all. 'Luc, sandstone cliffs are re-nowned for nasty surprises. You feel unsafe, you're out of there.'

'Leaving it to you? I don't think so.'

'Same goes for me,' Blake said grimly. 'By the look of that car they might already all be dead and I want no more bodies on my watch. Har-riet's proof of what these cliffs can do. Watch your backs, people. Watch everything. Let's go.'

They landed and they hardly talked. Blake and Luc had fitted part of their gear in the chopper but it had to be checked and rechecked before they went near the edge.

'Anyone hear anything from the car?' Blake demanded.

'Nothing.' The chief of the local fire crew, a woman in her fifties who'd introduced herself brusquely as Carol, had things under control. Or as much under control as she could. 'The husband says Tess has her phone on her but it's rung out. I won't let anyone try again. If she's unconscious, if any of the kids try to wiggle to answer it...' She let the sentence hang.

'The abseilers?'

'Friends of our local cop,' Carol said. 'Seems they did a course a couple of years back. Rex called them out but they seemed so nervous I pulled them back.'

'Well done,' Blake said gruffly.

'And you guys can do it?'

'Piece of cake,' Luc said. 'In our sleep.' He was adjusting his Prusik loop, the extra loop linking the main rope to the harness. The loop was sometimes referred to as dead man's handle, an essential backup safety measure. He looped it around his rope and attached it to his carabiner. Making sure he locked it. 'Those cranes you mentioned?'

'They'll be here any second. You get cables down, we'll stabilise.'

'Check?' Blake said.

There was another safety measure, checking each other's equipment, double checking locks were secure. Blake and Luc checked each other, and Sam did her own check for good measure. She checked Blake first, reaching for the metal loop attaching Blake's belay plate to the centre of his harness.

And then, almost as if it was part of the checking process, almost as if it was part of their normal, professional routine, Sam reached up and kissed Blake, swift, hard on the mouth. It was done almost before it began, before anyone could notice.

But Luc had noticed.

Sam and Blake were practically joined at the hip, Luc knew, a tight-knit couple who worked brilliantly as a team. And for just a moment, as Sam turned to check his locks, he felt a pang of longing so great it threatened to overwhelm him.

If Beth was here…

Right. If Beth was here, in low light, with her gammy leg, there'd be no way he could concentrate properly. All his attention would be on her, when it had to be on the job at hand.

How could Sam bear Blake to take risks? And vice versa? To watch someone you loved walk into peril…

It was far better to be like he was. Alone. Worrying about no one.

He needed no one.

And then a guy broke away from the group clustered around the police car. A big, burly guy in his forties, seemingly capable, steady, intent, and headed towards Luc.

'I'm Mike,' he muttered as he reached him, and he grabbed Luc's hand in his own vast paw. 'It's my family down there.'

'We're doing what we can,' Luc said. And then he added, 'We're good. If anyone can get them out, we will.'

Carol came up and took his arm to lead him away, but the man wasn't going anywhere. 'My Tess's sensible,' he told Luc. 'She'll keep her head. The kids... Zoe and Robbie'll do as they're told, though Robbie'll cling to Tess. Tom...he's a tense kid and he freezes. But tell him there's a fire engine up top of the cliff and he'll do what you want.'

'That's useful,' Luc said, nodding at Blake to make sure he'd heard it in the wind.

Once more Carol tugged, but the man still had hold of Luc's arm. And the rigid control he'd used to convey information seemed to snap. Capable? Steady? Not so much. This was a man crumbling under a pressure so great it was destroying him.

'Bring 'em back to me,' he said. 'I can't... Tess

and I…we've been dating since we were seventeen. She's bossy and independent and she drives me nuts but hell…' His voice broke on a sob. 'My family… They're all I need in the world. Tess is all…all that I am. Please…please bring them up safe for me.'

Every nerve-ending, every last fraction of his concentration had to be on the job at hand.

The two local abseilers, plus Gina and Sam, were up top, controlling their lines, making sure any slip wouldn't turn into disaster. He and Blake were descending toward separate sides of the car.

But it wasn't easy, or maybe that was an understatement. The cliff face was crumbling sandstone, and the closer Luc got to the ledge the worse the situation seemed. The nose of the car was almost completely crumpled, and it rested with a tiny percentage of the mangled metal on the ledge.

If he or Blake dislodged any more of the already smashed cliff face…

They couldn't. He had to concentrate on handholds. On trying to find a fraction of rock on which to place his feet.

If it had been a sheer drop it would have been easier, just belaying them both down. But the rocks jutted out just enough to make that impossible.

So concentrate…

And he was, but there was an echo in his head that wouldn't go away.

'*They're all I need in the world.*'

And while he concentrated he thought…that's what he wanted Beth to feel. That she needed him more than anything.

But not the other way around?

Why was he thinking that now? How did he have room to think it? But it was in his head and it wouldn't go away.

How would she be feeling if she could see him now?

And then he thought of all the times he'd done this job or rescues like it. If he and Beth had stayed married… He would have expected her to stay home and be safe and yet still…need?

The anguish of the guy on the clifftop stayed with him.

She's bossy and independent and she drives me nuts but hell...' His voice had broken on a sob. *'She's all I am.'*

How would he feel if Beth was in this car?

Gutted. Exactly how the guy up top was feeling.

But what if it was the other way around? If Beth knew where he was right now...

She did know. On some subconscious level he knew that she knew. Not that he was hanging over a wild ocean, trying to get into a wrecked car, but she'd know he'd be doing something like it.

He'd place her in a cocoon of safety and not let her care?

'This isn't working.' Blake's voice came through his headphones, strained to the limit. 'I'll have to bail. The car's hit these rocks on the way down and they're already dislodged. It's threatening to shift more. I'll head back up, try and descend further across and come at it laterally. How about you?'

'Still okay.'

The thoughts of Beth were still there but they

weren't taking his concentration from the job at hand. Rather they were heightening his senses.

She'd done this sort of work, too. She'd told him about the car wreck she'd crawled into. At the memorial service a couple of locals had spoken of it in awe.

He'd have tried to prevent it.

So he had double to prove, he thought, as he fought to find the next toehold. He had to save these guys for themselves. But also...for Beth?

He had a sudden vision of Beth as he'd first met her, fiery, funny, independent and supremely talented.

She still had that. Sure, she'd lost an edge to her physical ability but as he finally found a toehold, he thought Beth would have found it, too. By feel.

Who needed fifty-fifty vision if you were Beth?

And all of a sudden it was like she was with him. His Beth. Part of him.

What had the guy said?

She's all I am.

'It's teamwork over here,' he muttered to

Blake, searching for the next toehold. 'We have it covered.

'We?'

'You have Sam up top, guiding us every step of the way. But somehow… I have Beth right down here, telling me what to do, and bossy doesn't begin to describe it.'

'Are you okay?' Blake said cautiously.

'Yeah, I'm okay,' Luc told him. 'More than okay. I seem to be operating on an epiphany and who needs anything else in the face of such a thing?'

'Cables would be good. Plus medical gear. Plus…'

'Yeah, right,' Luc said, almost cheerfully. He was operating at full strength now, doing what he was good at, every nerve tuned to the job at hand. 'But don't you mess with my epiphany because it seems to be right what I need, right when I need it. You go on up, mate, and stay safe. I'm almost there.'

And then he was there. Not on the ledge itself—some things were a no-brainer—but to the side, hanging from his harness.

Every impulse was to drop further so he could

see through the smashed windows into the car but he'd worked in enough situations like this to put instinct aside.

He hovered, toes gripping the cliff just above the car. Steadied.

'Cables,' he muttered, and Sam—or Blake or whoever was at the top of the cliff—attached the first of the steel cables and lowered it down, hooked to his mainstay.

He caught it and then rode his harness in a seated position until he had it fastened under the passenger-side rear-wheel brace.

One. It wouldn't hold.

'Next?'

He could almost taste the tension emanating from the top of the cliff.

Another cable snaked down.

He fought his way across the top—or base—of the car and attached the cable to the rear driver's side.

'You got something up there holding?' he asked.

'Two ruddy great tow trucks parked well back.' It was Sam's voice. 'Blake's trying again but having trouble. More cables?'

He wanted to see what was in the car. If anyone was conscious they must be able to hear him work but there'd been silence.

Were they all dead?

But he had to work on, on the assumption there were people who needed to be saved. At the very least he'd prevent the car—and any bodies—from plunging into the sea.

She's all I am.

The guy's voice was echoing, messing with his head.

And Beth, she was in there, too.

She's all I am.

'Two more cables to be sure,' he muttered, and forced himself to be still and wait until the cables had run down, until he had four hawsers hooked across the car chassis, until he felt the guys up top gently, gently take up the slack so the car wasn't going anywhere.

'Done.' Sam's voice came through his earpiece. 'She's as secure on this end as we can make it. Cables secure?'

She wasn't asking if the cables themselves were fastened. She was asking if the body of the car was still intact enough to hold together.

'Looks as good as we can make it. Keep the pressure up.' It should be okay. From underneath the chassis looked solid.

Time to edge sideways and down a bit.

Time to look through those smashed windows...

He took the pressure from his stay and slipped downward, using the ledge now to steady himself. No weight, though. If the ledge itself crashed the car could still swing...

The rear window was smashed into crystallised glass. He could see nothing.

Down further...

She's all I am.

Beth.

This wasn't Beth. This wasn't personal.

Only it was. Every fibre of his being was pleading...

He had himself secure. He swung around— and a woman was looking out at him. Straight at him through the gap in the smashed glass. Clear-eyed. Conscious.

Alive.

'Tess,' he said, and he saw her face sag, just for a moment. And then some sort of iron control reasserted itself. 'I'm Luc,' he told her. 'And I'm very pleased to see you.'

'You…you took your time.'

'There was a small matter of tying your car up so it wouldn't slip further,' he told her, keeping his voice calm, pragmatic, workmanlike. Emotion right now would help no one. 'There are now four cables attaching you to cranes on top of the cliff. The car's going nowhere. You're safe. We just need to get you out. The kids…'

'I think…' He could hear pain in her voice, and the numbness of shock, but she had herself in hand. 'They're all in the back. Zoe says…. Zoe says Tom's knee's been bleeding—a lot—but she's wound her windcheater round it and tied it. She says the bleeding's slowed. I wasn't game to move… I thought…' She caught herself and he could hear the effort she was making to stay calm. 'I told the kids…if we stay really, really still even if we hurt, even if we're scared, then Santa will be so impressed he'll bring double this year. Isn't that right, Zoe?'

'And we did.' A girl's voice, much shakier than her mother's, piped up from the back seat. 'I'm cuddling Tom and Robbie.'

'You know what you are?' Luc said, and for some reason he was having trouble keeping his own voice steady. 'You're a heroine, Miss Zoe. And so's your mum. And you boys...if you can hold on just a little bit longer... There's a fire engine up on the cliff and if you manage to stay still until we take you, one by one, up the cliff in a harness, then you'll officially be heroes in fire hats. The fire chief will give you all helmets.' They'd probably dock the expense from his pay but what the heck.

'Fire helmets...' That was a quavery voice, very young. Not much older than Toby.

Oh, God, Toby...

'It's a promise,' he said, very solemnly, and then Blake was slithering down beside him and tools were being lowered to prise the doors open.

She's all I am.

Suddenly that line was front and centre. He wanted to tell Beth. He needed to tell her.

And in that moment he accepted what he'd been fighting now for so many years.

He needed.

He needed Beth.

* * *

'Margie?'

Her phone rang just as she finished morning clinic. The call was from Margie, the head of childcare at Namborra. She saw the name appear on the screen and felt a huge tug of regret. 'Hey, it's lovely to hear from you.'

'Good to hear your voice, too, Beth, love,' Margie told her, but there was a strain in her voice that said this wasn't a social call.

And that brought back the niggle of disquiet. For the last twenty-four hours she'd been fretting...about Luc? Stupidly fretting. There'd been no basis for worry but for some reason she thought...she *knew* that all wasn't well with Luc.

She'd almost rung him but sense had held her back. She was being irrational. Imagining things.

And now... Margie was in Namborra. She'd hardly be ringing about Luc, but the tingle of fear remained. And she'd definitely heard tension in Margie's voice.

'Margie, what's wrong?'

'I didn't... We shouldn't ask.'

'You shouldn't ask what?'

'You're in Brisbane, right? And back at work?'

'Yes.' If you could call it work—fielding requests for scripts from city dwellers popping in to see if the new doctor was an easy target.

'So if I said...we needed you...'

'What's happened?' The fear for Luc was acute—which was dumb but she couldn't get rid of it.

'It's Maryanne.'

Maryanne. She who ruled the medical kingdom of Namborra.

'What's wrong with Maryanne?'

'She's had a stroke,' Margie told her. 'Luckily she was in the hospital when it happened but of course there wasn't even another doctor. They called in the med. evacuation team from Bondi Bayside. They took her to Sydney last night but they're saying it's serious. One of the nurses here knows someone who works at Bondi and they're saying there's left-sided weakness, possible neurological damage. It's...it's too soon to say but best guess is that she'll be looking at months before she's back at work. If ever. And now... there's no one.'

Margie paused. 'Beth, love, we don't know

where you're up to, medically, and we know Maryanne didn't trust you to work on your own, but there's not a soul in this district who doesn't trust you to care for them. Beth, would it be possible…just until we can work something out… would it be possible for you to come home?'

Home.

And there was only one answer it was possible to give.

She still had the niggle of fear for Luc but Luc didn't want her. Didn't need her.

Namborra needed her.

And I need to be needed, too, she said, but she said it silently and she was talking directly to Luc. *I can do this.*

'Of course I can,' she told Margie. 'I'll be there on the next plane.'

CHAPTER ELEVEN

THERE WERE INJURIES—of course there were—but for such an accident the outcome was almost miraculous. Some jobs were better than others, Luc thought as he watched the med. evacuation chopper take off toward Sydney. Blake and Sam were in the chopper but Luc had been left behind. With four patients, plus one tearful, almost unbelievingly thankful husband and father, the chopper was full. Gina would take Luc back in the smaller chopper, but they had to collect their gear first, plus fill in whatever the local rescue services needed to get their reports right.

Normally Luc followed the steps fast and efficiently. Tonight, though, he left Gina to it. He stood on the clifftop and stared out to sea, and Gina had the sensitivity to leave him be.

He was shaking. He, Luc, who never got emotionally involved, was shaking.

There'd been broken ribs. A fractured arm.

Multiple lacerations. The accident had been caused by failed brakes, a truck on the wrong side of the road. An ambulance had taken the truck driver to the local hospital, suffering from shock.

'The brakes failed. I put my foot down and there was nothing there. I couldn't get the gears to hold it. There was nothing I could do, and I could have killed them.'

He hadn't, because one woman had had the sense to keep calm, stay absolutely still and somehow talk her kids into doing the same.

Tess's purse had been in the footwell of the passenger compartment. How tempting would it have been to lean over and fish for her phone, so she could get some contact to the outside world.

She hadn't. She'd assessed the situation and decided the risk was too great.

Beth would do that, Luc thought. Beth was just like Tess, a practical, sensible woman who wouldn't crack in a crisis.

He thought of her calmly holding Toby under her T-shirt in the concrete rubble, waiting for help. Knowing it would come.

Knowing he'd come?

How could she?

He thought of Sam and Blake tonight—Sam deferring to Blake's overall command, watching Blake abseil into danger. Staying on the clifftop, ensuring both Blake and Luc stayed secure, feeding equipment down the lines. He and Blake had both needed Sam.

The cliff where Blake had been trying to descend had crumbled—he knew that now. Sam must have felt it as Blake had lurched, as the line had gone taut with strain, but there'd been no panic. Blake depending on Sam's skill to keep them safe.

And there was a deeper level. Sam depended on Blake.

Their wedding was to take place in two weeks. It was a marriage of equals and Luc knew in his bones that they'd be gloriously happy.

They needed…each other.

There was a touch on his arm and he turned to find Gina watching him, looking worried. Gina was an amazing chopper pilot and they depended on her absolutely.

They needed Gina.

He was thinking suddenly of his mother, fragile, brittle, demanding. She'd needed, over and over again.

She'd even needed her little niece's death to be his fault, so she and her sister wouldn't have to take the blame.

'It wasn't fair.' He said it out loud and Gina's look of concern deepened.

'Luc, love? Are you okay? You did great. Really great but everyone's safe. Thanks to you.

'Thanks to all of us.'

'We're a great team,' she said, and suddenly she hugged him. 'Come on, mate. Let's go home.'

'Back to Bondi?'

'Where else?'

'I'm not sure,' he said slowly. 'Yeah, for now, Bondi. But home… Hell, Gina, I've never had one.'

'Hey, I've seen the view from your apartment.' He had her seriously worried—he could see that. 'Your home's amazing.'

'The telly's too small.'

'Really? You can fix that.'

'I might have to,' he said slowly and then, because she was still looking worried and she was part of his team and he loved every single one of them, he hugged her back. 'But that's for to-morrow. For now…you're right, let's go home. Wherever home is.'

The commercial flight from Brisbane to Namborra left at ten the next morning and Beth was on it. With Toby.

The head of the clinic had been annoyed when she'd rung to quit, but not surprised. He was a man in his seventies, an entrepreneur who wanted to make money from medicine.

'I knew you wouldn't stay,' he said gruffly into the phone. 'You guys who want to save the world drive me nuts. Me, I just want a quiet life making a decent nest egg for retirement.'

A decent nest egg. She thought of the fortune the man was reputed to have and she almost choked.

'So I'm heading to Namborra, the outback town the plane crashed into a few weeks ago,' she told him, and then cheekily added, 'You want to make a donation to the rebuild fund?'

'You're telling me I'm losing a doctor to them—and you want money?'

'Would you rather donate money or come and do the hard yards with me?'

And amazingly he'd chuckled, and promised a bank transfer.

That was great but as soon as she disconnected she stopped thinking about him. About Brisbane. She had to get on that plane. She had time to think of nothing else.

Except… Luc was still in her mind. In her heart?

Why had she been worried last night? Why the niggle?

For that's all he is, she told herself firmly as she carried Toby up the steps onto the plane. 'A niggle. My life's about to get very busy and that's just the way we want it. We have no time to worry about Luc. We're on our own again, Toby, love.'

She was about to be Namborra's only doctor.

That was taking alone to a whole new level.

Luc had a couple of minor scratches that needed attention—hauling kids and mum one at a time out of the wrecked car and harnessing them up the cliff had involved a scratch or two. Blake insisted on a full body check and told him to go home to bed.

As if he could. He showered and checked again on his rescued family—all present and correct—and then headed up to annoy Harriet.

'Hey, well done,' she told him. 'The guys are saying you did good.'

'It's the mum who did good,' he told her. 'Having the presence of mind to freeze and get the kids to stay frozen…they saved themselves.'

'So that dressing I see on your hand…'

'I gotta have something to show for a night's work.'

'It sounds as if it was awesome. Oh, I wish I'd been with you.'

'I know you do.' He stooped and hugged her. 'But your rehab is going great. You'll be back as part of the team…'

'You know my leg won't let me,' she said, flatly now. 'You're mouthing platitudes, Luc Braxton. Me and Beth. Perfect or nothing, and perfect's not going to happen. And if we're not perfect then you can't take it. You'll spend your life worrying about us.'

'That's…'

'True,' she finished for him. She put her head to one side and considered. 'Tell me I'm wrong then. You don't want to wrap Beth in cotton wool?'

'I… What she does is her business.'

'So if she ever decided she wanted to hang from ropes and save people?'

'She'd never be able to.' It was a gut response, and he saw Harriet wince.

'Yeah, like me. No rope hanging for us because we're *not* perfect.'

'Harry…'

'It's okay. I understand.' She tugged his hand so he had to stoop and then she hugged him, hiding her face for a moment in his shoulder. Using the moment to regroup? 'I'll just…figure it out. My way. I hope.' She moved back and seemed to have herself back under control. 'By the way, have you been in contact with Beth?'

'I… No. Why should I?'

'Why not indeed,' she said speculatively.

'There's nothing wrong?'

'There you go again. Protective mode.'

'I'm not.'

'Yeah, you are.'

He held up his hands in surrender. 'Okay, Harry, I admit it. I messed up our marriage. I love her. I…' He stopped. How to say it. But in the end it just happened. 'I need her.'

'Even if she doesn't need you.'

'She's proved she doesn't need me.'

'She might.'

And panic slammed back. 'What…? Harriet, what are you…?'

'It's okay. There's nothing wrong,' she said hastily. 'Or not with Beth.'

'Toby…'

'Will you stop it? If you're going to be any use at all, you need to get over that mind set.'

He paused. Took a breath. Eyed Harriet with caution.

Yeah, he was overreacting. He needed to work on that.

He needed to work on a lot of things.

'So why are you asking if I've been in touch with Beth?' He flattened his voice. Tried to make himself sound only vaguely interested.

Failed.

'Because of Maryanne,' Harriet told him.

He had a feeling Harriet was playing games

with him and he needed to stay calm and ride it out.

'Maryanne.'

'Namborra's doctor.'

'That's who I thought you meant.' He hesitated. 'So… Maryanne… She hasn't cracked and offered Beth a job?'

'I don't know about the job but it seems she has cracked.' She was watching him, he thought, assessing his reaction. He felt like an insect in a specimen jar but there was nothing he could do about it.

'Explain,' he said sternly, and she took pity on him and did.

'She's ill,' she said. 'The med. evacuation chopper brought Maryanne herself in yesterday. Sue from the flying squad popped in to see me late last night. She knows Beth's from Namborra and she thought maybe I might let Beth know. I have Beth's number but… I thought I might wait. And talk to you.'

'The med. evacuation chopper brought Maryanne in…'

'Stroke,' she said, briefly, back in medical mode. 'She has some cognitive impairment, hopefully transient but it's too soon to tell. She's still in Intensive Care and of course that means Namborra's without a single doctor. Anyway, it occurred to me that if your Beth found out about it…'

'She will have.'

'Yeah?'

'She has friends at Namborra. Of course they'll tell her.'

'There you go, then. No need for me to tell her. No need for you to even contact her.' But she was looking at him again in that same way. Head to the side. Inquisitive.

Summing up the possibilities.

What were the possibilities?

There was little love lost between Beth and Maryanne. He knew Beth would be concerned but he doubted she'd be rushing back to Sydney to see her.

But then…

He thought of Namborra, of how remote it was, of how long they'd taken to find doctors in the past, so long in fact that Maryanne had had to accept Beth and Ron.

He thought of how Beth felt about Namborra. She'd given but…she'd felt the community cared.

There it was again. She'd needed Namborra and Namborra needed her.

'Hell,' he said, and saw Harriet's curiosity step up a notch.

'Hell? Really?'

'She'll go.'

'That's what I thought,' Harriet said in satisfaction.

'She can't.'

'She can't what?'

'You know as well as I do. She can't cope on her own.'

'Because?'

And he took a deep breath and fell silent. He walked over to the window. Now Harriet was in permanent rehab, she'd been moved to one of the few rooms in the hospital with a sea view. He could see the bay. He could see…

The future. Beth working her butt off in Namborra.

Bringing up Toby alone.

The urge to fly to the rescue was almost overwhelming.

But…

She wouldn't want him.

He wanted her.

'Luc?' Harriet's voice from behind him was almost tentative. 'What are you thinking?'

'I don't know,' he said, and he didn't. 'But… hell, Harry, I need to go take a walk. A very long walk. I think… I think I have a whole lot of thinking to do. A lifetime's worth of thinking and that may take quite some time.'

CHAPTER TWELVE

BETH'S DAY HAD been crazy, from beginning to end. It had started at three in the morning with a false alarm: *'I was sure it was a heart attack, Doc—Stevie told me I shoulda let that curry alone...'* She'd been running on catch-up all day. And now, when she should be heading home for dinner, she was stuck in a bathtub with a three-year-old.

It sucked.

There wasn't a lot of choice, though. Three-year-old James Hollis trusted her. His mum, Millie, was eight months pregnant and had finally been persuaded to take a few minutes out and give her body a rest. Someone had to sit in the bath with her little boy.

For James Hollis's toe was firmly stuck in the plughole.

Beth had given James as much tranquilliser as

she dared but he didn't seem sleepy. He was bundled in blankets and pillows. She was holding him tucked into her. His toe was inconveniently stuck but she'd given him a digital nerve block. He wasn't upset. They were watching some ridiculous cartoon about a cute wombat on Beth's laptop.

Walter Wombat's moralising antics were making Beth want to throw up.

She still had a ward round to do—plus when the firefighters currently cutting pipe under the house finally got James out of the bathtub there'd still be the not so small matter of giving anaesthetic while she cut the plug from his foot. She doubted he'd stay calm enough for her to do it under local.

And there was another worry. Anaesthesia. She needed to be two doctors.

She was currently weighing up sending James to Sydney—when they finally had him free—but that'd mean another hour at least with his toe constricted. Or do the thing herself?

And Toby... Margie had him in care and would be giving him dinner. He'd be having fun. He wouldn't be missing her but, oh, she was missing him.

'We're cutting through now,' one of the firemen called from under the house. 'We've got your end of the bath stable but don't move, Doc. We're cutting through the floorboards so we can see to cut the enamel from the side.'

'Fine,' she called back. James had headphones on—thankfully—so she didn't have to compete with a cartoon wombat telling her not to litter.

Her leg was aching. Of course it was. 'Stay off it as much as possible,' the orthopod back in Sydney had told her and she thought, yeah, right, she was off it. She was sitting in a nice bath at the end of a long day.

Joke.

'Done,' the voice from below said in satisfaction as she heard a clump of masonry fall away. 'Coming up. You respectable, Doc?'

Ha.

She sighed. Two weeks as Namborra's sole doctor and she was exhausted.

Two weeks and the rest of her life to go?

Without Luc.

Stop it. Stop-it-stop-it-stop-it.

The mantra in her head wasn't working but she had to make it work. She'd spent years teaching herself that she didn't need Luc, and here she was, pining like a teenager.

An uncomfortable teenager. In a bathtub.

But she couldn't keep doing this. Two weeks doing the work of three doctors had made her see sense. It wasn't fair to Toby.

It was impossible.

'The firemen are coming back in,' she told James, lifting a corner of his earphones. On her instructions, the firemen had donned their uniforms and were keeping them on. James had been told if he was very still then he and his mum could ride to the hospital in the fire truck as soon as he was free. It was pretty exciting for a three-year-old, and he was being extraordinarily good.

It was only Beth who wanted to drum her heels and yell.

Or weep.

She felt…she felt…

Like she had to get a grip. She did—sort of.

She held James tighter and put on a cheerful professional face as the door opened and a couple of firefighters trooped in.

And…oh, for heaven's sake…

Luc?

Luc. Here he was again, riding to her rescue, and it wasn't even Beth who had her toe stuck.

He was casually dressed. Faded jeans. Open-necked gingham shirt. Smiling?

At her.

The urge to weep was almost overwhelming.

She didn't, though. She sat in the bathtub and held James and didn't say anything at all.

'We've cut it right out.' Troy, the head of Namborra's fire service, sounded almost cheerful, talking over his shoulder to Luc. 'A great hunk of the floorboards and we've cut the pipe below. Once we rip these side tiles off we'll have full access—we'll cut that plug right out and they'll be free. This is young James Hollis. His mum's about to pop another baby out, his dad's doing a bit of interstate truck driving and James here decided he'd make life more interesting by sticking his toe in the plughole.'

Then Troy turned to her and the little boy she was holding. 'How you going, young James? Doc Carmichael? Here's Doc Braxton come to help. He's one of the docs who was here during the plane crash. You remember Doc Braxton, Doc? Hey, wasn't he the doc who came with you to the memorial service? Of course you know him.'

Of course she knew him.

She stared up at Luc in stupefaction. His smile had slipped. He was looking at her as if he saw the tears she was struggling to hold back.

He was looking at her with concern, with a look that said she'd be cared for and cherished...

Yeah, been there, done that, got the T-shirt.

'What are you doing here?' It was a snap, out before she could stop herself, and his smile returned.

'That's not a very polite way to greet a friend. Mind, greeting friends from bathtubs does put you at a disadvantage. I can see that. I stopped at the hospital and they told me I could find you here. So I thought I'd pop right over and help.'

Of course he did. That was what he did. Riding to the rescue. Luc, the hero.

She'd had it with heroes. Hadn't she made a decision to stay clear of this man? For ever?

But right now… It would be petty—and unprofessional to say she didn't need him.

As well as untrue.

'I… Great. Could you…could you check on Millie?' she said, grudgingly. 'I… She's thirty-seven weeks pregnant and she's been sitting in the bathtub for longer than I have.'

'Where is she?' And he'd clicked into medical mode, just like that. Which was also what he did. He was no longer Luc, her ex-husband, her nemesis. He was a colleague and right now she could have fallen on his chest and wept.

Only you didn't do that to…nemesises? Nemesi?

Maybe she was close to hysteria?

'I hope she's in her bedroom. I sent her there twenty minutes ago.'

'Right,' Luc said. 'But we might do a bit of role swapping?' And before she could argue, before she could say that James trusted her and might disintegrate with strangers around him, Luc was kneeling beside the bath and producing his phone.

James, who was finally wearying of Walter Wombat and his nauseous prosing, shoved back his headphones and looked at Luc with wobbly suspicion. The sedative was keeping him back from the edge of toddler panic, but he was reaching the limits of his endurance.

Any minute now he'd disintegrate.

'Hey, James. I'm Dr Braxton. I'm a doctor who's very good at getting toes out of plugholes,' Luc told him. 'But first, would you like to see what you look like?' And he lifted his phone, snapped a fast picture of James and handed the phone over.

What child could resist seeing a picture of himself? James stared at the screen, fascinated.

'Let's take a picture of Doc Carmichael holding you?' Luc said, and did, then gave the phone back to James.

Another moment. James's attention was totally caught.

'And now...' Luc said with all solemnity.

'We'll make a movie. Watch.' And he took the phone, stepped back and took a quick clip of Luc and Beth in the bath with Troy stooping to knock away the tiles.

'We can do even better,' Luc told him as he replayed it for James's benefit. 'If I hop into the bath we can make pictures of everything that's happening. I'll show you and then I'll teach you how.' He handed the phone to James and held out a hand to Beth, a hand that told her she was coming out of the bath right now.

So she could object—or she could do what he said.

It felt like giving in.

It felt like sense.

She went to push herself out but she wasn't permitted. He stooped, tugged her upright, then put his hands on her waist and lifted her bodily from the bath. Then he swept her against him and hugged, a brief, strong hug that had nothing to do with professional anything—but if they sold that sort of comfort in bottles…

Um…not. She'd be professional even if he wasn't.

'I… Thanks.' But he'd already released her and was sliding into the bath behind James, attention back on his phone.

'Now, James, we press this button. That lets us see ourselves in the camera. If we hold it right out here we can even see what the firemen are doing under the bath. You can hold it while we take pictures of just us, but if we want the firemen I might need to hold it because my arm's longer. Dr Carmichael, can you please go check on anyone else who needs checking? We'll call if we need you, won't we, James?'

'M-Mummy,' said James, uncertainly.

'Dr Carmichael's going to give your mummy a cuddle,' Luc told him. He'd been recording while he talked so now he turned the phone around and hit replay. 'And the firemen are going to get your toe free. James, I think you might need to wiggle your ears to make our picture more interesting. Can you wiggle your ears? I can. Why don't I wiggle and you hold the camera?'

And twenty minutes later one toe—with metal plug and James attached—was ensconced on the front bench seat of the fire engine. With Millie. Troy even obliged by using sirens and flashing lights as they headed for the hospital.

Luc followed in his car.

Beth followed in hers. Dazed.

Luc had his car. That meant he hadn't flown here.

It was half a day's drive from Sydney.

That meant...no flying visit?

Her mind was in overdrive. Here was Luc, dashing to her rescue again. She should tell him to turn around and go straight back to Sydney but of course she couldn't. She needed his professional help.

Nothing else.

Liar.

What was he doing here?

'Just rescuing,' she said wearily. 'Just being someone I need. Oh, Luc, how am I going to learn not to need you?'

With two doctors the procedure to remove one toe from one metal ring was relatively simple. Beth gave the anaesthetic, really light as James was already sedated. Once the adrenaline of the rescue and the fire engine ride was done he'd slumped into his mother's arms and hardly noticed as Beth had set up a drip and administered what she needed to put him under.

Luc did the actual removal of toe from metal. If the plug hadn't been so bulky he could have used an orthopaedic pin-cutter, but for this they needed heat shields to protect the underlying skin, then the specifically designed surgical cutter with grinder attachment.

And good eyesight.

Yeah, she could have done it, she conceded. Her magnifying glasses would have worked.

Except…she was bone weary. Her hands were starting to shake and the cutter required eye-watering precision. To be safe, she'd have had to send him to Sydney. Instead she monitored breathing and watched while Luc expertly freed one toe.

It was a five-minute job. The toe wasn't compromised. James surfaced from the anaesthetic and almost instantly drifted toward normal sleep.

There was swelling because of initial tugging,

but by tomorrow he'd have nothing more than a slightly sore toe, a memory of firefighters and fire engines—and a heap of pictures to show his dad when he got home.

One of the firefighters had stayed on to take Millie and James home. Beth walked out to the car park to see them off and then walked back inside.

To face Luc.

He was helping the nurses clear equipment, chatting as if he'd known them all their lives—and gently probing as to what else needed to be done tonight. For a moment she stood back in the doorway of Theatre and watched. Barb and Dottie were the nurses on duty—middle-aged, sensible women. The clearing was finished. Neither of them actually needed to be in Theatre any more but she could see they were attracted to Luc as moths to flame. She stood and watched and thought… Yeah, why wouldn't they be?

And then Luc turned and saw her. He smiled and she thought moths and flames had nothing on her.

'All done, Dr Carmichael?'

'Thanks to you,' she said, and was cross that her voice quavered a bit. 'I… Thank you.'

And Barb nudged Dottie and Dottie nudged Barb and they disappeared.

Which made her feel even more…even more she didn't know what.

'Think nothing of it,' he said, and his smile became a caress all on its own. And before she knew it, he was across the room, enfolding her into his arms and holding her tight.

Just…holding her. Nothing more. Just holding.

She could feel the beat of his heart. She could feel the strength of him.

Her Luc.

'Beth,' he whispered into her hair, and somehow it sounded like a vow.

She had things to do. She needed to move on. She needed to back away, thank him nicely for what he'd done, ask what the hell he was doing here, tell him she no longer needed him but it had been very nice of him to come check on her.

Instead she simply stood and let her heartbeat settle to his. And pretend for just this moment that this was how it could be.

Luc…

Her phone rang. Of course. Her phone had been ringing pretty much nonstop since she'd returned to Namborra. She'd flicked it off in the bathtub and then again as she'd put James under, but the moment she wasn't urgently needed, she'd flicked it on again, ready for the next problem. It was what she did.

Like Luc responding to need.

But instead of letting her answer, Luc lifted the phone from the back pocket of her jeans and answered it for her.

'Namborra Medical Service. Dr Braxton speaking.'

'Give it to me,' Beth tried, but he smiled down at her, used his spare arm to hug her even closer, and went on speaking.

'Right. I can see why you're worrying, but the incubation period for meningitis is well and truly over. If your little boy caught it from Felix he'd have had it by now. But tell me the symptoms.'

He listened, his face grave and attentive, but while he listened his fingers started playing with her spine. Doing…doing…

She should listen. She should…

Oh, the feel of those fingers…

'You know, that sounds very much like a cold to me. Thirty-seven point seven? Yes, that is a slight fever but it's very, very mild. And he has a runny nose? Is he alert? Did he eat his dinner? Yes, I agree we can't be too careful but I think, given the symptoms, that we can wait and watch for a while.

'What I'd like you to do is pop him in the bath—watch the plughole, by the way—there's been a bit of a problem with toes and plugholes and we don't want that to go around. Pop him in pyjama bottoms with no top and put him to bed as normal. Don't put too many covers on him. Take his temperature again before you go to bed and if it's over thirty-eight then I want you to ring me again. No, not Doc Carmichael. I'm the doctor on duty tonight but this number reaches us both. That's great. Get some sleep yourself and feel free to ring if you have any concerns. Goodnight.'

And he flipped the phone closed and tucked it back into her jeans pocket.

And she stared up at him, stunned. What had he just said?

'You're what?'

'What, love?' The fingers started their magic again. He was smiling down at her. Lovingly? Oh, Luc…

Back off. Back off! This was terrifying.

'You're the duty doctor tonight?' she managed.

'I thought I'd start tonight—if it's okay with you. I agree, as junior partner I should have asked you first, but seeing as I—'

'Junior partner… Luc, what are you doing?'

They were right by the sinks. She could feel the bench at her back. Luc was in front of her. The bench was behind.

The bench felt solid. Luc felt…terrifying.

'I'm here to stay,' he said, and even the bench stopped feeling solid.

'You can't.'

'I can't stay?'

'No.' She was hovering between tears and laughter. 'Luc, you know you can't. You'll go nuts. A family doctor…'

'I think I might like it.'

'You wouldn't. You won't.'

'Why not?'

'Because it's not dangerous,' she said, feeling desperate. 'Because it's not filled with adrenaline. Because you don't get to swing on ropes and dive into burning buildings.'

'No?' He appeared to think about it. 'You know, I've never considered family medicine until now, but I've spent a lot of the last couple of weeks talking to Maryanne. She sends her regards, by the way. They're pretty fuzzy regards. She has residual left-sided weakness so her speech is a bit impaired but she's fit enough to tell me exactly what this job involves. And why it's unsuitable for someone like you with a bit of sight impairment. Because she says there *are* times when you need to hang off ropes.'

'I never have…'

'But you crawl into wrecked cars. You head into unknown homes at the dead of night. Maryanne says you've talked people out of suicide. You watch kids grow, dealing with every dumb accident kids fall into. You cope with unexpected babies… Why is Millie still here, by the way? Are you seriously proposing to deliver her? No matter, we'll talk of that later. All I figure is that family medicine can be routine and I think I'm ready for that, but it also seems that it can be very exciting indeed. There'll be dramas here and we're first responders. Like stuck toes with fire engines attached. How can I return to Specialist Disaster Response and miss that?'

'You can't be serious.' She could hardly breathe. 'Luc, you can't. Honest, you'd go nuts.' She took a deep breath. 'I've figured…tonight in the bath I thought it through. You're right, I can't cope here on my own. It's not fair to anyone. Namborra will need to find someone else. I don't know who but it can't…it can't be me. And as for you coming here, too, you know it's impossible. You'll go crazy trying to stop me taking a fair share and I can't watch you go crazy. Luc, I don't need you that much.'

'No,' he said seriously. 'You don't. That's what I figured. It's taken me a while—ten years, in fact. I'm a slow learner but I have it now.' He took her by the waist again and tugged her into him, hard and strong. 'You don't need me that much but I need you at least that much. No. I need you more.'

'What…what…?'

He kissed her hair, a feather touch, a touch she should hardly have felt but it was a touch that sent shards of heat running through her entire body.

'I get it,' he said softly, into her hair. 'Finally…'

'You get…what?'

'That I need,' he murmured. 'That I've always needed. You know my background. You know my crazy mother. She was damaged herself and she spread that damage. I was only worth anything when I was needed. If I wasn't needed, I wasn't loved. I've done enough hard thinking over the past few weeks—in between fighting fire-breathing dragons—to accept that I need to change. But, then, I guess I've always known that. It's just that I haven't wanted to change enough to do it.'

Her heart was hammering but so was his. Two hearts beating as one. How corny was that?

She didn't do corny. She couldn't hope for

corny. Hearts and flowers? Violins playing soppy love songs?

Her heart was screaming, Yes, please.

But she needed to listen. She had to listen. Luc's voice was little more than a murmur and every nerve-ending was attuned to every syllable.

'I've spent the last ten years thinking you needed me,' he was saying, even softer now as if he could hardly believe what he was saying, as if there was some deep part of him surfacing that had to struggle past barriers that were a lifetime deep. 'But you know what? I've watched you dispatch dragons, and there hasn't been a single time when you haven't whirled and coped with your own threats.'

'That's not to say... I mean, there will be times...'

'When the dragons get too much?' He kissed her then, properly this time, and it was a kiss that was so sweet, so tender that she almost melted on the spot. 'Of course there will. Those dragons will be there for me, too, and when they are, I want you to be the one looking out for me. That's because I need you. But you know what I've finally figured? I love you first and need comes second. So, Beth, I'm hoping...no, I'm gambling my life here on the one big thing. That you love me regardless of need.'

She couldn't speak. She was having trouble breathing. She didn't...she wasn't...she couldn't respond.

But he hadn't finished. He had both her hands in his, smiling down at her in a way that made her heart turn over, that made joy build to a point where she felt she might turn into a puddle of happiness. That the world was somehow transforming into something new and bright and magnificent.

Listen, she told herself fiercely. Listen...and breathe.

'Beth, you have damaged eyesight and sometimes you need help,' he was saying, holding her tight. 'Right now you have a damaged leg so you need help there, too. Maryanne's desperate to get back to work but she'll probably be left with residual weakness and she'll need help as well. But maybe my disability is worse. Beth, I was a lonely kid who never got taught the basics of loving, and how does a little eyesight loss or leg injury or even left-sided weakness compare to that? It's huge. So of the three of us...'

'The three of us...'

'Yep,' he said in satisfaction. 'Because our future needs to include medicine. I've spent the last two weeks trying to sort this out. I needed to get all my ducks in a row before I talked to you. This isn't a half-baked idea, love. It's a full-blown rest-of-our-lives proposition. Maryanne wants to come back after rehab but she'll face restrictions. She knows that but she's accepting—very humbly, by the way—that if we give her space she can manage. That makes a country practice of three doctors. It'll be three doctors who all have different needs but, hey, no one's perfect. And maybe together we can provide what this town needs. And...what we all need?'

'I...' Where had her voice gone? The lone syllable came out a squeak and she had to breathe a few times before she could try again. 'Luc... are you talking medical practice here or...or us?'

'I'm not including Maryanne in the marriage,' he admitted, and he chuckled and drew her closer. 'But I am talking marriage. Seriously now. The way a man should talk marriage.'

He put her back from him then and held her at arm's length but his eyes still caressed her. 'For that's what this is all about,' he said softly. 'This is the single biggest thing I've ever said. We married once but I know now we married for all the wrong reasons. The love was there but there were too many ghosts. I hadn't sorted them—and maybe you hadn't sorted yours, either. But finally our ghosts seem to have been dispatched and I can't tell you how grateful I am. So...'

'S-so?'

'So, Beth Carmichael, I love you with all my heart. Would you do me the very great honour of marrying me? Properly this time, though, Beth. Marrying for love. Not for need, though need's there because, God knows, I need you more than life itself. But, Beth... I've never stopped feeling that you're my wife. I want to slay dragons with you, not for you. I want to have a family.

A dog? A brother or sister for Toby? I…whatever… Will you…?'

And he stopped. He could go no further.

And neither could she.

He was looking down at her with all the anxiety in the world. He didn't know, she thought. He didn't understand…

So say it, she told herself. Just say it.

One little word.

One vast, soaring ode to joy.

'Yes,' she said as he gathered her into him.

'Yes,' she said as he raised her and swung her round and round until her heart felt like it was swirling out of her body.

Yes, she said again, but this time her yes was silent because his mouth had found hers.

Because two people had found their home.

* * * * *

LET'S TALK

Romance

For exclusive extracts, competitions
and special offers, find us online:

f facebook.com/millsandboon

⧇ @millsandboonuk

🐦 @millsandboon

Or get in touch on 0844 844 1351*

For all the latest titles coming soon,
visit millsandboon.co.uk/nextmonth

*Calls cost 7p per minute plus your phone company's price per
minute access charge